I0527311

Henry James Byron

Dearer than Life

A Serio-Comic Drama

Henry James Byron

Dearer than Life
A Serio-Comic Drama

ISBN/EAN: 9783337342418

Printed in Europe, USA, Canada, Australia, Japan

Cover: Foto ©Andreas Hilbeck / pixelio.de

More available books at **www.hansebooks.com**

A Serio-Comic Drama,

IN THREE ACTS.

By HENRY J. BYRON, Esq.,

Author of " *£100,000,*" " *William Tell, with a Vengeance,*" " *Aladdin,*" *etc.*

AS FIRST PERFORMED AT THE ROYAL ALEXANDRA THEATRE, LIV-
ERPOOL, UNDER THE MANAGEMENT OF MR. E.
ENGLISH, NOVEMBER 25, 1867.

TO WHICH IS ADDED

A DESCRIPTION OF THE COSTUME—CAST OF THE CHARACTERS—EN-
TRANCES AND EXITS—RELATIVE POSITIONS OF THE PER-
FORMERS ON THE STAGE, AND THE WHOLE
OF THE STAGE BUSINESS.

NEW YORK:
ROBERT M. DE WITT, PUBLISHER,
NO, 33 ROSE STREET.

CAST OF CHARACTERS.

	Alexandra Theatre, Liverpool, Nov. 25, 1867.	*Queen's Theatre, London, Jan. 8, 1868.*	*Selwyn's Theatre, Boston, Mass., March 9, 1868. First time in America.*
Michael Garner.	Mr. J. L. TOOLE.	Mr. J. L. TOOLE.	Mr. G. H. GRIFFITHS.
Uncle Ben, his elder brother.	Mr. DAVID FISHER.	Mr. L. BROUGH.	Mr. H. PIERSON.
Charley, Michael's son	Mr. WARDROPPER.	Mr. C. WYNDHAM.	Mr. H. S. MURDOCH.
Bob Gassitt	Mr. ELDRED.	Mr. H. IRVING.	Mr. E. COLEMAN.
Old Bolter		Mr. C. LEYTON.	Mr. H. F. DALY.
Mr. Kedgely		Mr. JOHN CLAYTON.	Mr. C. STEDMAN.
Mr. Chigley			Mr. G. F. KENWAY.
Mr. Mingle			Mr. O. H. DINSMORE.
Mrs. Chigley			Mrs. T. GRAHAM.
Mrs. Garner	Mrs. DYAS.	Mrs. E. DYAS.	Miss A. HARRIS.
Lucy, her niece.	Miss ADA DYAS.	Miss H. HODSON.	Miss L. ANDERSON.
Mrs. Pellet	Mrs. PROCTOR.	Miss EVERARD.	Miss M. WILKINS.
Mrs. Mingle		Miss EWELL.	Mrs. STEELE.
Misses Chigley		Misses JORDAN and LEE.	Miss FORREST.
A Guest			

TIME OF PLAYING—TWO HOURS.

SYNOPSIS.

Michael Garner, a hard-working and honest tradesman, is about to celebrate the twenty-seventh anniversary of his wedding. His family consists of his wife, his son Charles, upon whom his mother doats with a blinded affection, and Lucy, his niece, betrothed to the young man. Charles has been covertly leading a dissipated life at the instigation of Gassitt, who aspires to marry Lucy. Charles' course of conduct is known to his father, who conceals it from his wife, fearing that exposure of her son's practices would break the mother's heart. Charles, losing a large sum of money on a race horse, makes Lucy a confidant, and ascertains from her that his mother has amassed a good sum of money through many years of saving, which she intends giving the young couple on their wedding day. This information is scarce imparted before Garner is visited by his son's employer, who charges that Charles has been guilty of forgery and embezzlement. Lucy induces Mrs. Garner to produce her money-box, in order to shield the young man from arrest, when it is discovered that that, too, has been robbed. Charles migrates to a distant country to retrieve his reputation and means, while the family are reduced to a point bordering upon starvation, in wretched lodgings, from which they are in danger of being evicted. Gassitt persecutes Lucy with his advances, and falsely represents Charles to have married abroad, while Garner, under the influence of drink, betrays to the mother knowledge of her son's misdeeds. The doating parent is prostrated, when Charles returns, a reformed and wealthy man, to claim his bride and to expose the iniquities of Gassitt, who has converted to his own use money remitted to his care by the absent Charles to support his father's family. Uncle Ben, an inveterate inebriate, smitten by remorse, avows the robbery of Mrs. Garner's money-box, and Charles emerges from suspicion, cleansed from all criminal taint.

SCENERY.

ACTS I. AND II.—Interior on three groves.

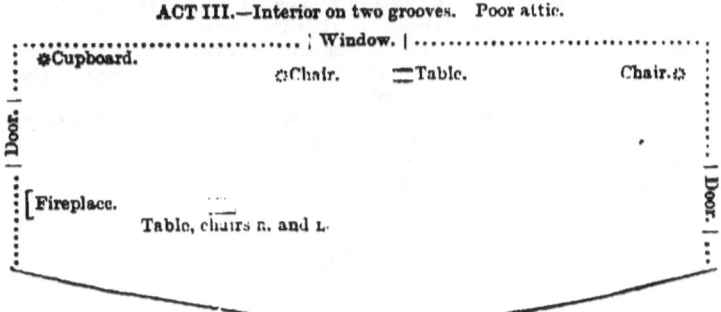

Carpet down. Closed in L. and R. A number of framed pictures on the flat and side-sets; white muslin net curtains to window in F., which is cut out.; D. in F. and in R. 1 E. set, practicable. Stairs R. are of four or five steps, leading up to platform and door; profile banisters on each side. Fire to burn in fireplace; basket of flowers and books on table R. front; cloth to same; chairs and sofa covered with a light flowered pattern chintz. Flowers and clock on mantel, L. 1 E. Chest of drawers, or side-board, up C., has a small strong-box on top of it.

ACT II.—The fire is burning. Very "comfortable" light interior.

ACT III.—Interior on two grooves. Poor attic.

Closed in R. and L. Naked appearance to the room; walls stained and cracked; some of the window-panes cut out, some broken, the rest dirty; backing to window view looking up a narrow street, house-tops shown; doors R. 2 E. and L. 1 E., practicable; fire to burn in fireplace, very feeble.

COSTUMES (*Modern, English.*)

MICHAEL GARNER.—*Act I.:* Made up a trifle stout and flushed of face. Light grey pants, white vest, blue coat with brass buttons, blue and black cravat, watch and chain, stand-up collar, eye-glass with black ribbon; black hat, red silk handkerchief; a letter in a wallet in his breast coat-pocket; light hair, short curl. *Act III.:* Drab pants, light faded vest, shoes, woolen tippet, black long-skirted coat, all very shabby; hat; hair a little long, disordered; pale face.

UNCLE BEN.—*Act I.:* Long-skirted coat of cheap, coarse stuff, blue overalls, black vest, some of the buttons off; neck-tie crooked, black skull-cap; long grey hair, white eyebrows, discolored face, hoarse voice. *Act III.:* Workhouse suit of dark blue serge; jacket, vest, loose trousers, shoes, cap, with peak; hair whiter than before.

CHARLEY.—*Acts I. and II.·* Grey trousers, with dark brown stripe down the seam; white vest, dark brown velvet cutaway coat, watch and chain; moustache (at pleasure). *Act III.:* Suit of black, long moustache and heavy beard; hat, black gloves.

BOB GASSITT.—*Acts I. and II.:* A sporting man. Black cutaway coat, black low-crowned hat, light brown pants, with black stripe down the seam; black vest, fancy neck-tie, with pin; bright metal buttons to vest and coat; watch and chain, fancy silver-mounted riding-whip; moustache (at pleasure). *Act III.:* Cane, suit of black, small black whiskers, hat, buckskin gloves.

OLD BOLTER.—Sea-captain's shore clothes, dark blue coat and vest with brass buttons; blue trousers, shoes, an old-fashioned hat, watch-chain, white neck-tie.

MR. KEDGELY.—Suit of black, white cravat, black gloves, sandy side-whiskers, grey wig, eye-glass, watch-chain.

A GUEST.—Suit of black; white tie, gloves.

MRS. GARNER.—*Acts I. and II.:* White cap (and a second one, very handsome, for *Act II.*); house-dress of color to suit. *Act III.:* Plain dress, hair down, or plain.

LUCY.—*Acts I. and II.:* White dress, with muslin over-skirt, with train; trimmed with narrow red crimped work; hair in fashion. *Act III.·* Hair plain, plain black dress, with collerette and cuffs.

MRS. PELLET.—Red dress, hair roughly put up; short sleeves to dress; face to look broad by arrangement of the hair, etc.; flushed; bullying manner.

MRS. MINGLE.—Old-fashioned dress, with muslin head-dress.

MISSES CHIGLEY.—Nice dresses, color to suit.

PROPERTIES (*See "Scenery."*)

Act I.: Whip for GASSITT; eye-glass for MICHAEL; cigar and matches (to light) in GASSITT's cigar-case; pipe (to break) for BEN. *Act II.:* Whip for GASSITT, as before; a newspaper; box of snuff for BOLTER. *Act III.:* Candle to burn; box of matches up C. on table; work-basket and dress for LUCY to sew; long pipe on mantel; letter for LUCY; cane for GASSITT; two cups and saucers, bread to be cut; knives, butter on plate, tea-pot, sugar-bowl, cupboard R. U. E. corner; bottle for BEN to bring on.

[*For Explanation of Stage Directions, see page* 34.]

DEARER THAN LIFE.

ACT I.

SCENE.—*Room in* GARNER'S *house, discovering* MRS. GARNER *seated* R. C., *front, by table,* LUCY *up* C. *a little.*

MRS. G. My dear Lucy, why have you not dressed yourself yet ? You are not going to receive the company like that ?

LUCY. Not I. But I must make the place look tidy a bit—it shall be quite grand ! (*down front,* C.)

MRS. G. Not too grand for you and Charley. You know that Michael and I are saving up a good round sum for Charley.

LUCY. Yes, Aunty. (*seated on foot-stool at* MRS. GARNER'S *feet.*)✓

MRS. G. What a pity that you cannot be dearer to me as my daughter, than as my niece. I don't let you want to see that—oh, I wish Charley would only show his affection half as well.

LUCY. The fact is, Charley is not very demonstrative.

MRS. G. That's just what I meant to say, my dear. You are good, and I love you, but Charley's very dear to me.

LUCY. Oh, Aunty, there's not a doubt of that.

MRS. G. (*kisses her*). Bless you for saying so ! There *is* not a doubt of it.

LUCY. And I am sure he loves you in return, and father, and his home. But he is certainly a little wild.

MRS. G. A—little—wild, but not wicked.

LUCY. Oh, no, not wicked—else we should not love him so dearly.

MRS. G. That's what it is, child. But then Charley is so young—it would not do to be too decided with him. Look at my cousin Ned Willoughby, as fine a young man as was ever seen in our village, but his old folks were so harsh upon him that, in reining him up quick, he broke from all restraint whatever, and went to the bad. Oh, if Charley were to take that course, it would break my heart—I should die ! I should die !

LUCY (*consolingly*). Oh, Aunty, there is no fear of that.

MRS. G. It is not to be thought of his becoming like Uncle Ben ; anything but that for my boy. But he ought to be here—he promised to come home early on the twenty-seventh anniversary of Michael's marriage.

LUCY. They may have kept him a little late at the office.

MRS. G. Or he may be with his friend, Mr. Gassitt.

LUCY. Aunty, there's something about that young man that I do not like. I wish Charley would not have anything to do with him.

MRS. G. No, child, I like him very well. He is such a good friend of my boy. (*rises.*)

LUCY (*aside*). I am not so sure of *that!* (*rises.*)

MRS. G. I must go up stairs and put on my new cap, that Charley was so thoughtful as to buy for me. A beautiful cap—almost too beautiful to wear! (*to stairs* R.) I'll be down directly—I'll be down directly. (*exit* R. *by stairs.*)

LUCY (C., *aside*) Dear Aunty, how she doats on her child! May no shadow ever darken this happy home. (C., *music.*)

Enter, D. in F., BOB GASSITT.

GASSITT (*aside*). There she is. (*comes down* L. C.) There's a girl to wear round your heart! there's a girl to take in your arms! (*aloud, hat off*) Here's Miss Lucy! I hope I am not in the way?

LUCY (*starts*). Mr. Gassitt here? (*quickly*) Charley is not in at present.

GASSITT. I don't mind stopping here for him. Charley don't appreciate his home's attractions like some others would. (*sings in a low tone*) Fol lol lol!

LUCY (*aside*). How annoying! I do detest this fellow.

GASSITT. Not that I wish he was altered in that respect.

LUCY. If there is any thing you want me to convey to him——

GASSITT. Now if you were a young lady (LUCY *starts*) I should ask you to convey something——(*sings as before,* fol lol lol, etc.) You twig?

LUCY. I do not understand your elegant phraseology.

GASSITT. Elegant phraseology! Here's good language, more fit for a gilded saloon than a back parlor! I meant, don't you understand? My language may not be tip-top, but I always speak my mind.

LUCY. Speak your mind? Then that's why you generally speak such rubbish! (*turns away.*)

GASSITT. Miss Lucy, don't go. I want a word with you.

LUCY. We are very busy to-day, sir, and——

GASSITT. I know! But I can't bear that you should be left in ignorance here. The fact is, you're superior to this sort of life! You were not "born to blush unseen and waste your sweetness on the" Old Kent Road! (C.)

LUCY. It's very kind of you to say so! (*aside*) Really, he is the most disagreeable young man I ever knew! (R. C.)

GASSITT (*aside*). I am evidently making an impression here! (*aloud*) Your friends are a good sort—Mr. and Mrs. Garner—and Charley, the old boy himself, is rather warm, eh?

LUCY (*aside*). I know I am getting so!

GASSITT. All very well in their way, but not what I call first-class! Why, even Charley is ashamed of them at times!

LUCY. Is he?

GASSITT. Yes!

LUCY (*fiercely*). Well, then, Charley has no cause to be ashamed of his parents, whatever he has of his friends.

GASSITT. You're a vitty vun, you are! Ha, ha! (*pause*) Do you ever go to the theatre?

LUCY (*shortly*). Why do you ask?

GASSITT. Why, I have got a friend who is a professional. He sometimes gives me an order. What would you say if I was to call round friendly-like and offer to take you! I'd square Charley. He prefers a game at billiards to spending the evening in an intellectual manner!

LUCY. Allow me, in the first place, to thank you for the generous way in which you have offered to "square" Charley.

GASSITT. Not at all!

LUCY. But let me add, that when I am taken to the play, I like to be paid for!' (*her tone growing more and more sarcastic*) If it is all the same to you, I prefer "an intellectual evening" at home! I dare say there are some young ladies who would take your invitation as an honor. When I call it an impertinence, attribute it to my want of taste!

[*Bow and exit* R. *by stairs.*

GASSITT. Ah! you stuck-up piece of fol-lal impudence! Who do you think you are, I should like to know? You suppose some young ladies would take my proposal as an honor? I should think they would! Why, you couldn't be grander if you owned a whole row of freehold cottages! There's nothing like landed property for fostering pride! That for your grand airs. (*snaps fingers, goes up* L. C.).

Enter R. *by stairs,* CHARLEY.

CHARLEY. Ah! are you there, Bob? (*puts his hat on side-board up* C.)

GASSITT (L. C., *up*). Yes. (*shortly.*)

CHARLEY. Talking to yourself?

GASSITT. Don't you mind who!

CHARLEY. Well, I don't!

GASSITT. Very well, then! I can see you are in one of your nice knock-me-down tempers to-day, Master Charley!

CHARLEY. What if I am, Master Bob?

GASSITT. Nothing; all the better! You couldn't be worse if you heard that Sunbeam is scratched!

CHARLEY. You don't mean he?

GASSITT (*carelessly*). The rumors are beginning to fly around. I shall hedge.

CHARLEY. They dare not have sold it!

GASSITT. All right, if *you* say they daren't! You are so uncommon sharp, you are. Accidents happen with the best-regulated horses, and I not being a *leg* used to being broken, like to stand on the safe side.

CHARLEY. If you have only come to talk nonsense, why——

GASSITT. Say it! Tell me to get out!

CHARLEY. No; I don't mean that. I've been troubled to-day. I'm all out of sorts. But what's put you out?

GASSITT. Well, the fact is, your fine-lady cousin, Miss Lucy, has behaved uncommon rude to me.

CHARLEY. It's the other way about, I guess.

GASSITT. There's some satisfaction when a man is impudent to you, 'cause you can punch his head.

CHARLEY. Well, suppose I'm the man, if you want to punch heads, and punch mine, if you can!

GASSITT. Hullo! Master Charley, are you coming the bounce, too?

CHARLEY. If I knew what it was you had been saying to her, I'd make you beg her pardon!

GASSITT. Make me beg—bah! I never begged any one's pardon in my life! Get out!

CHARLEY. Then, I'll make you beg now! (*seizes* GASSITT *by the throat.*)

Enter D. *in* L., MICHAEL GARNER.

GARNER. Hullo! hullo! hul—lo! boys, boys, boys! (GASSITT *and* CHARLEY *separate, and* GASSITT *goes to* L. *a little,* CHARLEY *to* R. C., MICHAEL *down* C.) Has Bedlam broke loose, or has the Thames set itself afire!

Come, come, you're not in earnest with your going into gymnastics? You're not in *sober* earnest?

GASSITT (*sullenly*). No, we were only in play, weren't we, Charley?

CHARLEY (*sullenly*). Only in play, that's all!

GARNER. Only in play? That's what the man said what kept the menagerie, what had the two rale Bengal tigers, that set to chawing one another on the floor of their cage. ' It's only their play!" he said, says he. It might have been hony their play, but as neither on 'em ever got up agin', it looked like earnest to the houtside public! Now, boys, what does the poetry say about it? "Let dogs delight," he says, "to bark and bite," he says; "but little children's hands," he says, "were never made," he says, "to punch each other's eyes," he says.

GASSITT (L. *by mantelpiece, contemptuously*). Yes, I learnt all that when I was a young 'un.

GARNER (*eyeglass up, looking at* GASSITT). When you was a young 'un! And an uncommon fine young 'un you must have been! A remarkably fine babby!

GASSITT. Why so?

GARNER. Why, don't you know that it's a regular thing that the men and women that was uncommon lovely in their babbyhood grow up into ugly ones, and wisey-wersy. Now it strikes me in that light, that you must have been a beauty when you were little!

GASSITT. Oh, if you are inclined to have a joke at my expense, I'll go——

GARNER (*changing his tone*). Oh, now! there's no one to take anything at any one's expense except mine, this day! This day is the anniversary of that when I married that young rascal's mother (*indicates* CHARLEY, R. *of him*) twenty-seven years ago! I want everybody to be pleasant and sociable this day.

GASSITT (*gives* GARNER *his hand*). I wish you many of them, old gentleman!

GARNER. Now, that's what I call hearty; ain't it Charley? But I say, you were really not in earnest that little while ago when I caught you at one another's throttles?

CHARLEY. How could you think it, father?

GARNER. Humph! There's one thing I should like. I should like to see you shake hands. If there's one thing in the world that's pleasant and agreeable, it's to see friends shaking hands. (*brings hands of* GASSITT *and* CHARLEY *together*.) There! doesn't that feel comfortable? You must promise us, as Charley's friend, that you will give us a look in?

GASSITT. Unless I have to attend to business.

GARNER. Business! Pshaw! I wont hear of the word on this day. Business! on the twenty-seventh anniversary of an intimate friend's father—no, of a father's intimate friends—no? of a son's father's—— Charley, help me out, won't you?

CHARLEY. I suppose you mean that you would like him to stop?

GARNER. That's the right thing. Not that we're very partial to you, but——Hem!

GARNER (*to* GASSITT). You will come? I can see by the look of your face that you can sing a good comic song, and there's a conumdrum and a riddle in the corner of your eye!

CHARLEY. You'll excuse me, father, but I don't think that Mr. Gassitt's riddles or songs would suit our company!

GASSITT (*carelessly*). Oh, dear, no! If you want any harmony, just ask Charley to contribute some of the verses with which he gratifies the choice spirits of the Convivial Coveys' Club every Friday evening! (*goes up* L.).

GARNER. Friday evening! Why, Charley, I thought you attended Monsieur Montalembert's French class every Friday night? (*to* GASSITT) Then you will look in?

GASSITT. Perhaps I shall. (*lounges up to* D. *in* F.).

GARNER (*goes up to* D. *in* F.). Put it plainer.

GASSITT. Very likely, then! (*Exit* D. *in* F.)

GARNER (*at* D. *in* F.). Don't put yourself out about it! (*comes down* C.) Where did you pick that fellow up, Charley? I don't like him.

CHARLEY. Oh, he's a little rough, father, but not a bad sort.

GARNER. I don't like your rough diamonds! What's the good of going through the world with a surly phiz to everybody? Whenever I come across one of these sullen parties, I says to myself: "My hearty, you may have a very sweet kernel, when one gets at it, but life is too short for Michael Garner to waste his time in cracking you!" I like to see cheerful looks and to hear pleasant words! more than all on to-day.

CHARLEY. I suppose that's a dig at me, because I don't go snickering about like a great girl! (R.) Oh, thank you for the hint.

GARNER. A hint! I never meant to give you a hint! Why, Charley, you know nothing could be further from me than any idea of giving you a hint!

CHARLEY. It is rather hard to find an enemy in one's own father! (*sullenly.*)

GARNER. An enemy—Char—(*checks himself, solemnly*) The only enemy you have is your ownself! You make me tell you—I did not want to say anything about it on a day like this—but here is a letter I received about you.

CHARLEY. A letter—about me—father? (*agitated.*)

GARNER. Hullo! What are you going into hysterics about? It ain't a warrant for murder or forgery?

CHARLEY (*aside*). Forgery!

GARNER. If I had known it was going to have such an effect upon you, I would not have produced it at all.

CHARLEY (*one hand on table, R. C., convulsively*). Let me know the worst! Would you torture me?

GARNER. Torture you! Torture you, Charley? What's all this high-flown talk for, when it's Mullins sent in his bill? He says if you don't pay for the tailoring he will go to the extremity of the law.

CHARLEY (*laughs, relieved, but forcedly*). Ha, ha, ha! the tailor! Is that all?

GARNER. Well, it may be a devilish good joke, but I can't see it!

CHARLEY. All this serious preamble about a tuppenny ha'penny tailor's bill! Ha, ha!

GARNER. A tupenny ha'penny! It's a bill that any swell in the land might be proud on! Forty-seven pounds odd——

CHARLEY. Pooh! Mullins had no business to send you the bill—he shan't have any more of *my* custom!

GARNER. Oh, *that's* right, then! That will happen which has happened so many times before; I will have to pay the bill! I know it, and I wont refuse; but when is this to stop, Charley? Fine clothes is not for the likes of you, and fast living should be left to, not our, but *the* BETTERS! See here, you've got so good a young woman awaiting for you when you determine to settle down and begin life in earnest. You have a mother whose only fault is that she loves you too well. I love you, too, but a mother's love is a precious thing—a religion in itself! When our two little ones were lost, and we had only you, we did not regret them so much, while you grew up lusty and strong. Charley, my son, on this twenty-seventh anniversary of the happiest day in all my life, make it brighter by promising to turn over a new leaf! I have kept ever so many reports of your ill conduct from your mother, who doats on you! I have told her many a falsehood for your sake; do let me now have the truth to tell of you! I implore you, I beg of you to change your life! Promise me! You can't want to break her heart and mine—hers, because you are to her dearer than life!

CHARLEY. Well, I don't know what I have done to deserve all this.

GARNER (with vehemence). Done! You don't know what you have done! You've broken my heart—that's what you have done! You've sullied the good name and fame I built up with a hard-working life! that's what you have done! You have made me live one long lie—telling your mother what you were not, while it choked me! That's what you have done! Oh, sir, I am speaking plain English! You've shown to me that you go to idleness—perhaps to crime!

CHARLEY. Crime!

GARNER. That's what you've done!

CHARLEY. These are harsh and bitter words, father!

GARNER. Truth is harsh and bitter! You've filled the cup to overflowing—drink of it as it comes.

CHARLEY. I work! I go to business like other young men——

GARNER. You go to business? Why if a shopboy of mine had behaved to me as you have to Crisp & Kedgeley, I'd—I'd have taken him by the scruff of the neck and flung him out of doors—aye, long ago! It is only out of respect for me that they have kept you up to now.

CHARLEY. I did think that we might pass over one happy day for once in a while—this was the last one I thought you would choose to pitch into me.

GARNER. Perhaps I have been rather violent, but, there! I'll try to think the best of you! don't let your mother know what has happened—it would spoil the day for her. Hush! she is coming. Laugh—look cheerful. I won't speak a word of it to her!

Enter, R. by stairs, MRS. GARNER.

MRS. GARNER. Ah! here is the truant. (embraces CHARLEY) My dear boy, I knew you could not keep away from us on such a day as this!

CHARLEY. Don't rumple my collar, please! I shall go out and have a smoke before the company comes.

MRS. GARNER. Not to fume the rooms? Oh, there's consideration for you! (R. C.)

GARNER. (L.). Charley, smoking is a very bad habit.

MRS. GARNER (fondly). Oh, let him, if he wants to!

CHARLEY (taking his hat up C., and lighting cigar). Oh, it's a mild thing, only a cigarette!

GARNER. A sickrette! What do they call it that for? because it makes you ill?

CHARLEY. I'll be back soon.   [Exit, carelessly, D. in F.

MRS. GARNER. Ah, Michael! he wasn't born for our line of life!

GARNER. I don't think he was, my dear!

MRS. GARNER. How very kind of him not to smoke his cigar in the room!

GARNER. Hem! he lighted it before he went out.

MRS. GARNER. We must humor him a little. You know, Michael, how we lost our two little ones.

GARNER. Yes, my dear! (C.)

MRS. G. And Charley's so delicate!

GARNER. Just as you please, my dear. Now, then, to be agreeable again! What do you say to somebody's investing his money in a present, all through remembering that this was the twenty-seventh anniversary of the marriage of a certain lady who shall be nameless for the present occasion? (*gives jewel case.*)

MRS. G. Oh! ain't they beautiful!

GARNER. I say, ain't it of a size, though? You have got your money's worth.

MRS. G. Magnificent!

GARNER. They're extra pressure, double-distilled diamonds, if you like!

MRS. G. And I do like!

GARNER. Now, who do you suppose found that for you?

MRS. G. Why——

GARNER (*eagerly*). Yes, yes.

MRS. G. Charley, of course!

GARNER. Eh? Oh, of course, of course! (*gayly.*) Wasn't it thoughtful of the young dog?

MRS. G. Dear Charley, he is ever so thoughtful!

GARNER. We were going along when we saw this splendid article in a jeweler's shop—a regular blaze in the window—endangering the insurance! Thinks I to myself, "Here's the old woman without any jewelry at home, when, why need she be?" so in I goes——

MRS. G. In Charley goes, you mean!

GARNER. Eh? oh, aye, in Charley goes, of course. He outs with his money, slaps it down, and the brooch was mine—Charley's I mean! So, here's strength to bear it, health to wear it, and wealth to get another one when it's gone! I'll go in to rig up, mother——

MRS. G. (*aside, musing*). My boy! ever good and kind and thoughtful—ah! (*by table, R. C., front.*)

GARNER (*aside*). She's not listening to a word I say! She is thinking of the dead little ones, and of our living hope, Charley, Charley! always Charley! (*at foot of stairs, R.*) She's in the clouds. My darling wife, may nothing ever shatter your idol—it would break your heart! No doubt of it, no doubt! [*Exit R. by stairs.*

Enter, D. in F., UNCLE BEN, coming down C., in a drunken state.

MRS. GARNER (*starts*). Oh, you here, Ben? Look here, wasn't it thoughtful of Charley to save up his money to buy me this beautiful present? (*gives BEN the jewel-case.*)

BEN (*maudlin*). So he's been wasting money on you, has he? Ah! you are all rolling in the lap of luxury, but you never think of making a present to your poor old nunkey. Nobody gives me a brooch. Nobody gives me anything. I wouldn't have nothing—except it was for what I took.

MRS. G. I am ashamed of you, Ben you know what to-day is, and that Michael particularly begged of you to keep sober and pleasant.

BEN. So I am sober (*hic*) and pleasant. (*smiles*) Is this real gold? (*brooch in hand*, MRS. GARNER *nods*) Boo'ful, boo'ful! What's it's use?

MRS. G. Use! why, it's an ornament, Ben.

BEN. Ah, nobody ever gives me an ornament.

MRS. G. I should think not, indeed. Why, Ben, you had a beautiful watch once—as large as a saucer, and what did you do with it?

BEN. Give it away.

MRS. G. Sold it for drink.

BEN Give me a try with this. I'll keep this!

MRS. G. Indeed you'll not; give it back to me!

BEN (*shifting brooch to left hand, farthest from* MRS. GARNER). No! it's time you gave me something.

MRS. G. Oh, very well, steal it then! It won't be the first time!

BEN. What do you mean?

MRS. G. You'll drive me to mention the many little things I have missed, just after you have paid us a visit.

BEN. Just for that, you shan't have it now.

MRS. G. Give me that back directly, sir! (*seizes* BEN's *wrists, struggle.*)

BEN. You would, would you, you vixen! Ah!

Enter CHARLEY, D. *in* F., *pushes* BEN, *who falls* L. *by fireplace, one arm on chair, and takes* MRS. GARNER *in his arms.*

CHARLEY. What does this mean, mother?

MRS. G. Oh, nothing of any consequence. (*picks up brooch and case, which have fallen.*)

BEN (*still down*). Strike me! strike me! pitch into my grey hairs! What's age, ungrateful young man, what's age, what's venerableness, what's decrepitation to you?

MRS. G. He's had too much again. Don't mind him, Charley.

CHARLEY. He's not had half enough. Look here, Mr. Ben Garner, when you can keep yourself moderately sober, we can tolerate your company. You are not in that condition now, so you had better go!

BEN (*rises*). So you turn me out—turn me out like a cur?

CHARLEY (*sneering*). Yes, very like a cur.

BEN (*working himself up into a passion till his final outburst at close of Act*). Very good! *you* dare to talk like that to your elder! you, a loafer, a scoundrel, a low, mean-spirited loafer! oh, let him come on and strike me again. You think him all that is good! the pink of perfection! ha, ha! Cling to your belief, cling to your idol, though he turns guiltily away. You've struck me, and all the drink in the world won't wash that out. If you stood in the dock and a word of mine could save you, I'd tear my tongue out rather than speak it. (CHARLEY, R. C., *confounded*, MRS. GARNER *paralyzed with terror*, C.) Love him still, now, if you can love him, trust in him! but I'll never forgive him—I'll never forgive him! I'll never forgive him. (*stands trembling out of breath, up* L. C.)

MICHAEL *and* LUCY *enter* R. *by stairs.* MICHAEL *throws* BEN *up* L. C. *and takes in his arms* MRS. GARNER, *who faints with a scream.* ALL *form picture.*

LUCY.*   * BEN.

MRS. G.*   * GARNER.

*

CHARLEY.   '   '

R. C.   C.   L. C.

CURTAIN.

ACT II.

SCENE.—*Same as Act I., discovering* LUCY *seated at table* R. C. *front,* CHARLEY L., *by fireplace.*

CHARLEY. We are the envy of our neighbors for our nice, quiet, happy home! They ought to have heard Uncle Ben.

LUCY (*gently*). There is a skeleton in every family, Charley.

CHARLEY. The skeleton needn't be always drunk!

LUCY. Oh, Charley!

CHARLEY. To come in and drive mother out of her wits with his drunken ravings. He's almost upset me for the day.

LUCY. There's something else troubles you, Charley. (*to* CHARLEY, L.)

CHARLEY. You're a good girl, Lucy; too good for me! Don't annoy me, though.

LUCY. What have you on your mind? I wish you would confide in me, Charley.

CHARLEY. There are some things, Lucy, which are not to be confided in another. Don't ask me more.

LUCY. I will not if you do not wish it; but (*hesitatingly*) is it money, Charley—a—a debt?

CHARLEY. Yes, yes, a debt—a heavier one than I can pay! (*half aside.*)

LUCY. I will leave you alone since you wish it, Charley. (*reluctantly going to foot of stairs,* R., *aside*) I half guessed his trouble. I'll surprise the whole secret next. I am going! [*Exit* R., *by stairs.*

CHARLEY (*by table,* R. C., *front*). I wear my disaster on my face. She reads it—she's so guileless and unsuspecting. Her sympathy tortures me. Oh, if I win this time, I'll give it all the go-by forever! If I lose—oh, that's not to be thought of! (*falls into chair, arms on table, sullenly thinking.*)

Enter, D. *in* F., GASSITT.

GASSITT (*coming down to* CHARLEY, *aside*). There he is in a pleasant fit! He can't have heard the news!

CHARLEY. I thought you were not going to come back.

GASSITT. "The wish was parent, Charley, to the thought!" Hem! Shakspeare! I wouldn't have come though, only I thought you had better hear the news.

CHARLEY. Something bad, by your manner.

GASSITT. Bad to some. Sunbeam is scratched!

CHARLEY. Then I am lost—lost—lost! (*falls into chair.*)

GASSITT. So am I! We're both in the same boat. We had best take care we shan't be found.

CHARLEY (*rises*). It's a swindle—a made-up affair! I'll never bet on a horse again! Fool that I am, it's just my luck! (*crosses to* L., *excitedly.*)

GASSITT. I wouldn't have fared any better if I had not hedged.

CHARLEY. It's the devil's money; no good ever came of it. (L., *by mantel.*)

GASSITT. (C.). Oh, if you've come to preaching and ride the high moral horse, I suppose you'll repudiate your little obligation to me!

CHARLEY. No! I owe it you, and I'll pay you. Only give me time.

GASSITT. Ah! time, eh? Time is money—you've had that of me—I can't give you both. I must go away. I have lost heavy sums. Somehow or other, all my knowing calculations have gone wrong. You have not done much of late to make me show you consideration. (*up* C., *lights cigar with match carelessly.*) You have often bled your father for yourself; now do as much again for your friend.

CHARLEY. My friend?

GASSITT. Yes, your friend, one that will stick to you, too, to the end!

CHARLEY (*gently*). Come, Bob, I have been worried more than you can think for lately. Let up a little on me.

GASSITT. Don't mind my ways—you ought to know me by this time. (*they shake hands.*)

CHARLEY. I ought to know you—(*aside*) but I don't.

GASSITT. Your father will be coming in directly. He'll do anything for you on such a day as this. Pitch into him while he is jolly; I'll look in again. (*at D. in F.*) Ta, ta! ta, ta!   [*Exit D. in F., lounging.*

CHARLEY (C.) My last hope knocked from under me. I believe this fellow's my evil genius! If it were not for him, I—oh, what a fool I have been. (*seated R. C., by table*) What a fool!

Enter LUCY by stairs, R.

LUCY. Charley! (*to* CHARLEY) There *is* something wrong. I wish you would trust me. A sorrow is only half a sorrow when it is shared with a friend. What is the matter?

CHARLEY. Don't ask me!

LUCY. But I *do* ask you! You are distressed on the very day when Uncle wants us all to be most happy. Tell me all.

CHARLEY. I dare not!

LUCY. I will be silent. Perhaps I can find you a way out of it.

CHARLEY. Not you!

LUCY. Is—is the—the amount of the debt very large?

CHARLEY. Overwhelming!

LUCY. Charley—you don't know that Aunty has been putting by a sum of money for me—for you and me—it is the savings for years—and such a large sum now! She would only be glad to save you pain, if she knew it, but she need not hear the truth. Suppose I was to get it for you.

CHARLEY. I may break my mother's heart—but I will not take the savings she has been putting together for you!

LUCY. For you—and me, Charley.

CHARLEY. No! that would only be adding to it another crime.

LUCY. Crime! I won't allow you to use such words, sir!

CHARLEY. Then again for the money to be of any use I must have it to-day.

LUCY. To-day! Oh, you *are* in a hurry, Master Charley. (*playfully*) I must tell Aunty, first, (R. *by foot of stairs*) and get the money from her. I'll say you are going to invest it in some company—that will magnify it immensely.

CHARLEY (*embraces her*). You are a good girl, Lucy—far too good for me. I wish that I had known—(*kisses her.*)

Enter, D. in F., GARNER.

GARNER. Ah, ha, ha, ha! I see you. Go on with it—I'll turn my head the other way. (*comes down* C.) If you do have any of it left, Miss Lucy, let me be customer number two. (LUCY *kisses him*) Ah! there's an appetizer! talk of your sherry and bitters, and your tonic invigorators! oh! it quite takes one's breath away! (*puts his hat on sideboard, up* C.)

LUCY (*to* R. *to* CHARLEY). I'll be back soon, with it!

                    [*Exit R. by stairs.*

GARNER. Ah! there's a girl you'd have to look far and near for the match to, without running against very sudden. There's not a girl in the neighborhood fit to hold a candle to her. She s one of those girls—(L. C.)

CHARLEY (R., *impatiently*). She is—she is——

GARNER. I say, she is one of those girls——

CHARLEY. Exactly so! she's——

GARNER. Well, perhaps, on the twenty-seventh anniversary, an event which was mainly the means of introducing you to the public, you will permit your father to finish his observation. You are all the time correcting me in my manners—but I don't think your gentility has much to brag on! It puts me in mind of the modern young lady's complexion—it's more put on than natural.

CHARLEY. Do look over it! You know how I have caught it from all quarters to-day.

GARNER. Then it's all blown over. Why, your mother has forgotten that dreadful scene of old Ben's ravings, and believes it was only his drunken talk.

CHARLEY. Uncle Ben! I wonder you permit him to come here—the broken-down old reprobate.

GARNER Let me tell you that Uncle Ben was once as fine a young fellow as ever stepped; but he was dragged down to what you seen him now, all along of bad company.

CHARLEY. I wish, then, he'd stick to his company and leave us alone.

GARNER. But time's getting on. We must titivate ourselves a little for the company. (*looks at watch*) Bolter ought to be here. He generally is oncommon punctual.

CHARLEY. Is Bolter coming?

GARNER. I should rather think he was a-coming!

CHARLEY. The rough sea captain with the boisterous voice—beginning speeches he never finishes and songs that never have an end.

GARNER. Well, you amuse me, Charley. Why, Bolter is generally invited out on account of his voice.

CHARLEY. I wish somebody had invited him out to-day!

GARNER. There's Mrs. Mingle—you haven't anything to say of her?

CHARLEY. No more than she has of herself! She sit talk of an evening with only one speech to each cup of tea.

GARNER. Let me tell you I knew Mrs. Mingle when she was a remarkably fine young woman.

CHARLEY. What a pity she did not continue so.

GARNER. Well, you do amuse me!

CHARLEY. Anybody else coming?

GARNER. To be sure, there's the Miss Chigleys——

CHARLEY. Oh! the Misses Chigley, a pair of little milk-and-water chits who have just life enough to make matters worse by trying to ape good breeding.

GARNER. Well, you *really* do amuse me, Charley! You couldn't carry it on better if you were the emperor of all the Russias or the man what wrote the Etiquette book. I don't mind it, but, as the little boy said, whose mother kep' a lodging-house, when the first floor, as was a posture maker, took to balancing the table on the tip of his nose—the wonder is, "How you keep it up?"

Enter, D. in F., BOLTER; *in a rough, hearty way comes to take* GARNER's *hand.*

BOLTER. Here he is, and he's brought himself all along with him.

GARNER. I hope I see you well.

BOLTER. The same to you, an I many on 'em!

GARNER. Thank you, old boy! I know you mean it!

BOLTER. How many does it make of 'em now?

GARNER. Twenty-seven!

BOLTER. No!

GARNER. Fact!

BOLTER. Young man, (to CHARLEY) when you come to being married twenty-seven times——

GARNER (laughing). Married twenty-seven times! ho, ho!

BOLTER. Yes, married twenty-seven years——

CHARLEY (R.). Well, when I am——

BOLTER. What? Eh! Oh, he's fairly frightened the rest of it out of me. Hang me if I know what I was going to say! (takes snuff.)

GARNER (to CHARLEY). Don't catch him up so, don't catch him up!

Enter, R., *by stairs*, MRS. GARNER *and* LUCY. *Enter*, D. *in* F., MRS. MINGLE, *the* CHIGLEYS, *and the* GUEST, *who are received by* LUCY. MRS. MIN-GLE *takes seat* L., *by fire.**

MRS. GARNER (to BOLTER). Why, Harry Bolter, how are you? (shakes hands.)

BOTLER. Is this you, on the twenty-seventh anniversary. Why, I wouldn't have known you! You're getting younger and younger every day! You're improving, mum! actually improving, mum! In a manner of speaking (catches CHARLEY'S eye, which confuses him) In a—a—manner of—of—speaking——

CHARLEY (half aside). In a manner of breaking down, I should say!

GARNER. Ha, ha! he's a sort of a wit, Charley is! (to CHARLEY, crossing R.) Don't catch him up so! He's an old friend, and I won't have him catched up!

BOLTER. On the occasion, mum, I've brought you a little present. (gives box.)

MRS. GARNER. How sweet! Oh, Harry Bolter, you were always an extravagant young fellow. (crosses L., to show box to MRS. MINGLE and LUCY.)

BOLTER. It's not much, mum, but the value of a present is made more by the spirit that prompts the making it.

GARNER. A very pretty sentiment! With your beautiful flow of language, Bolter, my boy, you ought to have married long ago!

BOLTER. Ah, Michael, the only woman I ever cared for you know all about.

GARNER (chuckling). Yes, I cut you out, you old hunks! Do you remember the fight we had behind the cowshed when I gave you the black eye, and you told the clergyman that you got it by running your face against the handle of the pump! (he and BOLTER laugh together.) Do you know I can't help think we were happier together, when poor boys, in the purer, better air of the country, than ever after when we had come up to the great noisy city to make our fortunes?

BOLTER (shakes hands with GARNER). Not a doubt on it, Michael, not a doubt!

CHARLEY (merrily). I should think men of experience like you were above the common error, long ago exploded, of rustic simplicity!

GARNER (aside to CHARLEY). Don't catch him up!

GUEST—CHIGLEYS (at back.)
LUCY.

CHARLEY. MRS. GARNER. BOLTER. GARNER. MRS. MINGLE.
R. C. C. L. C. L.

CHARLEY. Ain't innocence in our sisters here as it was in our mothers down there? Don't a country dog hold on when he's gripped like a town-bred one? Of course he does! Ain't one just as good as the other? (*half aside*) I'm ashamed of you!

GARNER (*to* CHARLEY). I tell you I won't have him catched up! (*to* BOLTER, *soothingly*) This is the way sons talk to their fathers in this nineteenth century!

BOLTER. Yes, they do, if we permit them. (*aside, looking at* CHARLEY) That's for you, young man! (*takes snuff.*)

GARNER (*takes snuff*). Is this some of the same rare old?

BOLTER. The same old, Michael! It'll last our time! (*offers box to* CHARLEY *politely.*)

CHARLEY (*takes snuff with distaste*). Why do you persist in offering people such abominable stuff?

Enter, D. *in* F., GASSITT, *lounging down* L. C.

BOLTER. Abomi—— (*checks himself*) I should think, my young sir, you could be more civil to an old friend.

CHARLEY (*contemptuously*). An old friend—of my father!

BOLTER. Yes, your father's old friend! For you to be ashamed of *them*, your friends must be a decidedly superior lot. (*turns and finds* GASSITT *at his left side*) This, I should say, was one of them. (*pause.*)

GASSITT. Well, old gentleman, I hope you will know me next time?

BOLTER (*emphatically*). Next time? I beg your pardon, I don't *know* you now! (*goes up* C. *to converse with others*)

GASSITT (*aside*). Well, this is about the nicest house I ever went into. I never come without being insulted.

CHARLEY (*to* GASSITT). I see, you couldn't stay away.

GASSITT (*insolently*). On second thoughts, I thought I'd keep an eye on you. (*up* C., *and lounges up to* R. *with* CHARLEY; *they converse, note-book in play, etc.*)

GARNER (*comes down* C., *jovially*). What's the next move on the board?

LUCY. I move that we adjourn to the dining room.

GARNER. Yes, there's lemonade and sherry and what you like for a sharpener before the meal; but don't spoil your appetites. Sally and Lucy have been out-doing themselves for the spread to-day.

BOLTER. Oh! I've brought my appetite. I think it but a poor compliment to go out to a dinner without one.

MRS. MINGLE (*waking up*). I say so, too!

GARNER. Well for you, ma'am! (*to* BOLTER) And then we'll have all the old songs—Poor Tom Bowling, the Death of Nelson——

BOLTER. I've got them all—I'm in capital voice, and I've made a new verse to the Honest Man.

GARNER. A new verse to the—(*eagerly to* MRS. GARNER) Do you hear that, Sally! Bolter's gone and made a new verse to the Honest Man! Why, it wouldn't seem like the twenty-seventh anniversary at all, unless we had the Honest Man! How does it go? (*laughable attempt to get at a tune by "la-la-la-ing" at it*) La, la, la, etc.

BOLTER. No, that's not it. (*begins to hum tune*)

GARNER. Oh! give us a verse of it—plenty of time before dinner is ready. A sort of rehearsal.

ALL. Oh, do, Mr. Bolter. (BOLTER *sings* with feeling*)

* CHARLEY.	GASSITT.	GUEST.	MISS CHIGLEY.
LUCY.	MRS. G.	BOLTER.	GARNER.	MRS. M.
R.	R. C.	C.	L. C.	L.

THE HONEST MAN.

1. They may talk about health, They may brag about wealth, Of re -

lations so fine and so grand.. But much better by far, Than those

at -tributes are, Is the grasp of an honest   hand.... For

money is spent, And it's lost, and it's lent, And confirm that remark many

can. Lies may lay on the lip, But there's truth in the grip, Of the

mf

. CHORUS.

grasp of an honest man. For money is spent, And it's

lost, and it's lent, And confirm that remark many can, Lies may hang on the

mf

lip, But there's truth in the grip, Of the grasp of an honest man.

II.

When one's in the world, and invectives are hurl'd at your head by your
    friends and your foes :
Then you find at that time, to be poor is a crime, a worse one than you
    would suppose ;
When you're poverty's slave, there's to make you feel brave, and your
    flickering courage to fan,
Why you'll find beyond price is the grip, like a vise in the grasp of an
    honest man.

                                        (*shakes* GARNER'S *hand.*)

GARNER. Now, then, all together !

CHORUS.

When you re poverty's slave, there's to make you feel brave and your
    flickering courage to fan,
Why you'll find beyond price is the grip, like a vise in the grasp of an
    honest man.

During the ritornelle of the accompaniment, GARNER *arranges the* GUESTS *by
    twos.*

GARNER. There you are! you with this lady. (GUEST and MRS MIN-
GLE. GASSITT *and* CHARLEY *keep up* R. *All the others exeunt* R. *by stairs,
gayly.*)
GARNER. Now, then, secure your ladies for dinner. You'll have time
for something sweet to clear your throat, Bolter.

BOLTER. I want nothing; was I ever in better voice?

GARNER. Why, there's nobody left for you. Here, take my arm! (*they go arm-in-arm to* R. *Sings*) "Firm is the grip, the grasp of an honest man!" [*They exeunt* R., *by stairs. Music dies away.*

CHARLEY. That song grates on my nerves! (*seated,* R. C., *by table, thinking*) If I do not arrange it to-day, all will be discovered to-morrow. What shall I do?

Enter, D. *in* F., GASSITT.

GASSITT (*aside*). They're all gone, are they? (*comes to* CHARLEY, *taps him on the left shoulder as a police officer does*) Wake up!

CHARLEY (*starts up*). Ha! what's that? (*recognizes* GASSITT) You!

GASSITT. You start as if you were took for felony.

CHARLEY. Felony? What do you mean?

GASSITT. Nothing. What should a friend mean? You ought to know me by this time.

CHARLEY. I ought to know you, but I don't. (*goes to* R., *at foot of stairs*) Well, will you join us? [*Exit by stairs.*

GASSITT (*aside*). Join you! I'd rather part you any day! You marry Lucy! Not if I can prevent it! I wonder what makes me think so much of her? I never did of any other girl. Somehow or other, beside her I feel like a regular low, common fellow! She's something superior, quite above me. Ah! Lucy, the day you make a happy man of Charley Garner, you'll make a broken-hearted one of Bob Gassitt. (C.) But you're not married yet, not yet!

Enter, D. *in* F., KEDGELY.

KEDGELY. I beg your pardon, is Mr. Garner in?

GASSITT. No, sir! (*aside, surprised*) Mr. Kedgely! It must be something uncommon to bring him here at such a time! (*aloud*) Unless your business is particular, Mr. Garner would hardly like to be disturbed.

KEDGELY. It is very important.

GASSITT. They are celebrating an anniversary of the old people's wedding.

KEDGELY. Poor old man!

GASSITT. It's no business that I could do for you?

KEDGELY. No! Be so good as to tell Mr. Garner at once that I must see him.

GASSITT (*aside*). It's some scrape Charley's got into, I'll stand to win on! (*aloud*) Is it a message I can give? Is it anything I can do?

KEDGELY. Yes, there is one thing you can much oblige my by——

GASSITT. And it is——

KEDGELY. To get out! (*looks* GASSITT *in the eye, and* GASSITT *turns away,* R.

Enter, R., *by stairs,* GARNER, *gayly.*

GARNER. Mr. Gassitt, we are one short at the dinner-table, and—— (*comes down stairs, aside*) Mr. Kedgely, here!

KEDGELY (*takes* GARNER's *hand, half aside*). My poor friend! (C.)

GASSITT. (*at* D. *at head of stairs, aside.*) Now for it! (*listens there awhile, then exits.*)

KEDGELY. Now, that that highly objectionable young man has gone, I will come at once to the point, Mr. Garner. I want to talk with you——

GARNER. Yes, sir. (*aside*) My boy's master. I really feel quite trembling without knowing why.

KEDGELY. You can leave the company of your friends for a few minutes?

GARNER. Yes, sir, for a few—few minutes, sir. (*agitated*.)

KEDGELY (*hand on* GARNER's *shoulder, kindly*). My poor old friend, prepare yourself for a great shock.

GARNER. Not—Charley?

KEDGELY. Charley! You know that we have had, at various times, to make complaints of him.

GARNER. I know it, sir. And I know your kindness to him. But I have had a talk with him on this day—the anniversary of his dear mother's marriage. He is much improved; he really *is* improving! he is very contrite.

KEDGELY. Would that I could think so.

GARNER. Don't you think so, sir? Oh, for the sake of his mother, do try to think so! Give him another trial. We were all young once, and did our little follies. Try him again, sir—you'll find him really improved. Then, if he does wrong you can be as stern with him as you like.

KEDGELY. Little follies! Mr. Garner, I can give it no other name than crime.

GARNER (*indignant*). Crime! Mr. Kedgely, don't use that word to my boy! Find another name, sir, find another name!

KEDGELY. I fully sympathize with you, my poor friend.

GARNER. My poor son!

KEDGELY. Out of respect for you, whom we know to be an honest man, we placed your son in a position of trust, where large sums of money passed through his hands——

GARNER. Break it to me gently, sir, gently, if you can! (*represses his sobs with efforts*.)

KEDGELY. He had orders to pay a large sum to Messrs. Dean & Fotheringay—and he never paid it. Harsh as the word may be, there is no other but forgery and embezzlement for such a double act of dishonesty.

GARNER. My boy, my poor boy!

KEDGELY. No one could regret more than I the sad duty I have been compelled to perform. It is a great blow—but you must bear it, my poor friend, you must bear it. I will leave you now, to compose yourself. Let it be a consolation to you that you have won a name for honesty and probity which none may excel!   [*Exit*, D. *in* F.

GARNER (*tearfully*). It has come at last! Bad company, and idle ways have done their wicked work! My boy, my Charley—he has broken his father's heart! (*falls into chair*, L. C.) he has broken my heart! (*sobbing*.)

Enter, R. *by stairs*, LUCY.

LUCY. Uncle, what is the matter with you?

GARNER. Lucy! (*without looking up*) go tell Charley I want to speak with him. Don't let his mother hear you.

LUCY (*going* R., *surprised, aside*). How unlucky poor Charley is. (*lightly*) However, I've got him the money!   [*Exit* R., *by stairs*.

GARNER. He must go away from here—go far away, and his mother must know nothing about it. It would kill her—it would kill her!

CHARLEY *enters* R., *by stairs, unsuspectingly*.

CHARLEY. Did you want me, father? (*to* O. R., *side of* GARNER, *who remains seated, not looking at* CHARLEY.)

GARNER (*in a tearful voice*). Yes, Charley, I—I want to tell you some bad news. You must go away from here—anywhere out of this place! All is discovered! You must escape! You are accused of forgery——

CHARLEY. Forgery! It is false!

GARNER (*rises, with joy*). Stick to that, Charley, stick to that, and I'll tell Kedgely he lied. (c.)

CHARLEY. Kedgely! (*hangs his head*, R. C.)

GARNER. It is true, then, it is true! (*sadly—pause*.)

CHARLEY (*abruptly*). Father! (*falls into* GARNER'S *arms*.)

GARNER. Charley, Charley! (*pause*) There's not a moment to be lost. They may be coming to arrest you, and who could keep it from your mother then?

CHARLEY. I will go. Father, I am not as bad as I seem. I was tempted into it by bad companions. Bob Gassitt was my evil genius from the first. If this had not been discovered, I would have repaid it—I had the means of doing so. I have not been so bad. Don't tell mother!

[*Music.*

GARNER (*determinedly*). She shall never know it!

CHARLEY. Anything but that! (*going* R., *with his hat.*)

GARNER. No, not that way! By the other door! I'll give you money to get away——

CHARLEY (*at* D. *in* F.) I will begin a new life! Kiss mother for me! Say something to Lucy! I will make no promises. You shall hear of me as a better man, if I live. Good-bye! (*very tearful voice*) God bless you! [*Exit*, D. *in* F.—*Music kept up, piano.*

GARNER. Charley! (*totters up* C. *to* D. *in* F., *looks off at open door*) Charley, my boy, my darling boy! Gone! (*comes down* C.; *door closes*) Gone! God forgive him! (*clasps his hands, very faint voice*) God forgive him! (*sinks into chair*, L. C.)

LUCY *enters* R. *by stairs.*

LUCY. What's the matter, Uncle?

GARNER. Lucy, don't leave me.

KEDGELY, *enters* D. *in* F.*

GARNER (*to* LUCY). Take hold of my hand; don't let go of it! A great blow has fallen on us——

LUCY (*aside*). Charley!

GARNER. On me! We were not so well off as you always thought.

LUCY. What are you saying, Uncle?

GARNER. I risked too much in rash speculations. I hoped to have paid my losses honestly, but, in an evil hour, I took the money of my old employers——

KEDGELY. You, Michael Garner!

GARNER (*not looking up*). I took the money, I forged the receipt! I—only I—have brought shame and disgrace upon this happy home!

LUCY. Mr. Kedgely, you will not proceed any further in this matter? I am sure there is some mistake. The money is here.

Enter, R. *by stairs*, MRS. GARNER.

Oh, Aunty! the money *is* here, isn't it?

LUCY.	GARNER.	KEDGELY.
C.	L. C.	L.

MRS. GÀRNER (*is surprised*). The money is here—but—Michael, what is the matter?

LUCY. Nothing! (*impatiently*) the money—the money!

MRS. GARNER (*tries to open box on sideboard up* C.) Here, here! the money is here, eh? Oh, it has been broken open; the lock won't work!

GARNER. The money! What money?

MRS. GARNER (*still trying to open box*). You know, Michael, the money we have been saving up against Lucy's and Charley's marriage. It is—(*opens box*) gone!

LUCY. Gone!

MRS. GARNER. It is stolen!

GARNER (*rises*). Stolen!

MRS. GARNER. Nobody knew where it was but you and me and Charley——

GARNER (*with grief and rage*). Charley! stolen by Charley! Oh, bitter shame. (BOLTER *and chorus sing the chorus of* "Honest Man," *softly. The accompaniment continues the ritornelle as curtain falls.*)

MRS. G.	LUCY.	GASSITT *enters* D. *in* F
GARNER.		KEDGELY
R. C.	C.	L. C.

SLOW CURTAIN.

— — —

ACT. III

SCENE.—*Garret in dwelling-house, gas down, candle lit on table* R.; *fire in fireplace,* R. 1 E. *set.* LUCY *discovered seated by table, sewing dress.*

LUCY. How weary I am of this work. (*sighs*) Ah! I wish I had a hundred hands to work them to the bone for poor Uncle Michael. What can he do, poor dear; what strength has he to compete with younger men? When I think of our old happy home, and Uncle looked up to as the most honest of men, oh! I feel sure that there was some horrid mistake! I can't believe it! Sometimes I think that it will all come right at last, and we can leave this dreadful place. Poor Aunty is a confirmed invalid, dying of a broken heart. And Charley, my promised husband, where are you? Not here, in your place, working for your parents. Alas! six months is gone since I last heard of him. Ah! (*pause*) I must get again to work. (*sews. Knock,* L. 1 E. D.) Come in!

Enter, L. 1 E., MRS. PELLET, *to* C.

LUCY. Oh, dear!

MRS. PELLET. Oh, dear! I should think it was, "oh dear!" a respectable housekeeper to be kept awaiting at a lodger's door for ever so long.

LUCY. I am very sorry. I did not hear you at first.

MRS. PELLET. Oh, don't give yourself any trouble! (*loftily*). I only came to tell you that there's a most respectable gent in the dog's-meat line as has been thinking of these rooms. He's in a large way, got his regular customers, and is punctual in his pay. So, if you haven't settled by to-night——

Lucy. You would turn us out?

Mrs. Pellet. There's no other all-turn-ative!

Lucy. You have a heart! We have been unfortunate, but——

Mrs. Pellet. The rooms or the money——

Lucy. Surely, you are too despondent, Mrs. Pellet. Your house is always full, and the other lodgers cannot be, *I suppose*, like us——

Mrs. Pellet. Oh, do you? Then you're jist mistook! My landlord expecks his rent as reg'lar as clockwork, but the lodgers have no feeling for a poor lone woman. Once I had a husband as good as the best, and a house as grand as the finest, but, as my first-floor lodger says, where are we now?

Lucy. If you will only give us a little time, we will endeavor——

Mrs. Pellet. Oh, I can't be put off any more with your wheedling ways! soft words won't pay the rates. I pays my way, and I expects others to act accordingly. I repeat, *(stamps foot)* I pays my way!

Lucy. I know what you are alluding to, ma'am. Where should we go, if you were to be so hard.

Mrs. Pellet. Go? why to the workhouse—like that poor old broken-down bloke who comes to visit you sometimes.

Lucy. Shame!

Mrs. Pellet. Why shame? what else is the work-house for, but them as can't pay their way?

Lucy. Woman! I forbid you to address me in this way!

Mrs. Pellet. You forbid? Woman! I should like to know who you are calling a woman! I'm no more of a woman than you are. I'm a respectable housekeeper, as pays my way!

Lucy. You shall be paid to-night, ma'am. In the meantime I request that you will withdraw.

Mrs. Pellet. Young woman, pride will be your ruin! Why, ain't there as good-looking a young man as the world ever saw, only awaiting for you to say the word, when he'll marry you.

Lucy *(rises)*. How dare you?

Mrs. P. Oh, I know all about it. Mr. Gassitt is only too willing to help your old folks, but you're too proud! He's got a bold way about him, that would have made even me think him quite out of the common, when I was of your age!

Lucy. Mr. Gassitt has no heart, and would only intrude on our misery. You can prevent him. Do not let him in, I order you!

Mrs. P. Oh, dear me!

Lucy *(submissively)*. I beg of you!

Mrs. P. *(aside)*. And him giving me my regulars to be let in! *(aloud)* Mr. Gassitt is such a bold young man, that perhaps he won't mind my telling him. We shall see. *(goes L.)* Mind you, I want my rent or my rooms! Them's Sarah Pellet's sentiments, and she sticks to them! *(bangs L. 1 E. D. open with fist, stamps her foot)* and she sticks to them! [*Exit violently.*

Lucy. Oh, poor weak creature that I am, what shall I do? We have really come to the last step. Ah! I must finish this to-night. *(seated as before)* To work, to work! *(sews a little, then leans her head on her arms weeping, on table, lifts her head)* I cannot work! *(produces letter from her bosom, unfolds it on table)* Charley's last. *(reads)* "Heaven bless all at home. I hope soon to be with you. It is very sad out here, all alone, but I pray for help, and I hope I shall come back a changed man, by repentance and labor. Out here, away from the noisy city, I see all the iniquity of my crime—there I did not feel that it even was a crime."

Enter L., GASSITT, *cane under arm, comes over* R. C., *looks at what* LUCY *is reading, smiles, recedes a little to* C. *up, aside.*

"By God's mercy I shall return worthy of you all."

GASSITT. Hem!

LUCY (*starts*). You here?

GASSITT. Reading something of interest, may I inquire?

LUCY. Something of the highest interest.

GASSITT. A letter—from Charley? (LUCY *nods coldly*) Ah, poor Charley!

LUCY. Poor, indeed! if he has sunk so low as to merit your pity.

GASSITT. Ah! Is there nothing, Miss Lucy, that I can do to make you look more favorably on me? I am not going to give it up so easily. (*crosses to* R. *side of table*) You're all in distress—next door to starvation; but a word from your lips would lift you out of it. I am not such a bad fellow. Lucy, I would go through fire and water for you. There's not a thing in the world I would not do to prove it!

LUCY (*coldly*). You know that Charley——

GASSITT. Charley! Oh, I know. I know all about it; more than his mother does. What would she give to be undeceived?

LUCY. Do you threaten?

GASSITT. No—not unless you force me to it.

LUCY. It would kill her! Through all our troubles she has been kept ignorant of her son's error.

GASSITT (*laughs*). Error! Call it by its right name, and say crime! Come, there's nothing in my power that you shall not have. I have got an appointment abroad. (*sits on table*) A party in the wine trade who appreciates my manners (*leans across table towards* LUCY) and business talents, has given me a berth. It ain't much, but it will help to something better, I hope. Say the word and you can leave the old people comfortable. (*with his face close to* LUCY's) Lucy, give a fellow a bit of a chance—just a little, least bit.

LUCY (*rises*). Robert Gassitt, I am the promised wife of Charles Garner.

GASSITT (*goes to* C., *carelessly*). Well, there was something I did not want to speak about yet, but you drive me to tell it. Lucy, you will never be the bride of Charles Garner.

LUCY. What do you mean?

GASSITT. Why, he is married already!

LUCY. It is false!

GASSITT. It is true! and if you won't believe me, there's Jack Willoughby who's come back by the last ship; he saw it all. Charley was down with the fever a long while, and *she* nursed him—— (LUCY *sobs, seated as before*) So that's the way. (*insinuatingly*) Oh, how could you expect steadiness of Charley—he was always flighty and changeable—never could settle long on one object. I didn't mean to tell you this until after you were Mrs. Gassitt—just to have some retort in store in case you should recall your model lover!

LUCY (*sobs*). Oh, oh!

GASSITT. Well, I'll leave you to think it over. Make it "yes," and they'll all be left comfortable; make it "no," and I don't know what you'll all come to! (*going up* L. C. *a little*) I'll look in again for your answer.

Voice of MICHAEL GARNER *heard off* L. 1. E., *singing. He enters* L. 1 E. D., *as if cold. His manner is the reverse of that in the previous Acts, being dejected and broken down.*

GARNER. Ha, ha! here we are at home again!

LUCY (*rises*). Uncle! (*kisses* GARNER.)

GASSITT (*aside*). Ah, Master Charley, I rather think I have settled your business. [*Exit quietly*, L. 1 E. D.

LUCY (*looking around*). Oh, where's——

GARNER. Where's what? (*at fire*, R.)

LUCY. Nothing, Uncle.

GARNER. It's not so werry cold when you're indoors. It's so very comfortable to see a fire. (*stamps his feet, checks himself*) It's not so werry cold. Oh! next I'll have the soles off.

LUCY. It has been snowing. Your feet must be damp.

GARNER. Damp! that's a good 'un. *My* feet damp! I'm not one of your cotton-wool chaps, that's afraid of a little snow. Where's Aunt, my girl?

LUCY. She was not very well, and she is asleep in her room.

GARNER (*half aside*). What will she wake to? what will she wake to? (*seated* R. *by fire*.)

LUCY (*aside*). To what indeed!

GARNER (*cheerfully*). I am getting on fust-rate in my new place. I didn't know I knew my way so well—rally so well. And Meadows Brothers sent me to the most out-of-the-way places I ever see. I'm regularly cut out for a messenger. When I was in business, I didn't take enough exercise—I'm making up for it now.

LUCY (*aside*). Lucy Garner! be a woman, and not a whimpering fool. (*aloud, rising*) Uncle, dear, won't you have your tea? (*gets tea-things from cupboard* R. U. E. *corner, and sets table.*)

GARNER. Well, I will, my dear, though I really wouldn't have thought of such a thing if you had not put it into my mind. I made a hearty meal late in the day—afraid you wouldn't think of waiting for me. It's such a long way to get to here—not too far! oh, dear no, not too far! and then it is so werry comfortable when you *are* here. I may say I rather like the walk. As Master Johnny says—he's oncommon fond of a joke—Master Johnny is, "I'm a rum 'un to look at, but a good 'un to go!" He's a merry chap, Master Johnny is. Ah! this is something like—pour us out a cup of tea! That'll warm one up!

LUCY (*pours out tea into* GARNER's *cup*). Poor Uncle, I knew you felt the weather. Your hand is quite cold.

GARNER. My hand is cold, is it? As long as the heart is warm, what does it matter? the extremities are not to be thought of. Ah, that cup of tea warms me again. Gently with the butter, my dear, gently with it. I'm of a bilious nature. (*mouthful*) Bread and scrape, my dear! bread and scrape! Well, really I am hungry, (*quickly*) notwithstanding the hearty meal I had late in the day! But (*suddenly*) you are not eating anything. Won't you keep me company?

LUCY. Thank you, Uncle, but I have no appetite.

GARNER Ah! Well, have you any more bad news? (*eating and drinking business continued*)

LUCY. Mrs. Pellet has been asking for her rent.

GARNER. Oh! has she been at it again, the old rammaulus? That for her. (*snaps his fingers*)

LUCY. She said she was going to let the rooms, and unless we paid the arrears she would turn us out!

GARNER. Pooh! She told me she would wait till the end of the week. By that time Bolter will be back. Bolter has a heart, and he'll help us. I've told him it was all a lie about my——

LUCY. All a lie? What do you mean?

GARNER (*coughs*). Eh! oh, a piece of bread gone down the wrong way.

(*takes up loaf*) Haven't you any more—is this all the bread in the house ?

LUCY. Yes, Uncle, until I get this dress done and take it home.

GARNER (*quickly*). I rally must have a pipe ! (*takes pipe from mantelpiece*) I rally must ! I feel such a longing for tobacco ! (*fills and lights pipe, aside*) It isn't the first smoke I've taken in place of food for a time past. (*gayiy*) But mother Pellet—bless her benevolent old countenance ! what did she have to say ?

LUCY. I told you, Uncle ! She knows you will have your wages of a Saturday night.

GARNER. My salary, my dear. Certain sums at a stated period are salary—plant that in your mind ! Then we'll pour the money into the voracious maw of mother Pellet ! How about Sunday's dinner ? What'll be the residue ?

LUCY. There's Aunty's medicine to be paid for.

GARNER. Aunty's medicine ! Bless me, I forgot ! True ! Oh, I've got an invitation out to dine on a Sunday ! Old Tom Matthews of our office —a most respectable old chap—often asked me to take dinner with him, and I really must oblige him. So I won't come home till late (*his voice has gradually wavered as if he was too tired to keep up the mock gayety. He sits, half bent over fire, smoking. Pause ; abruptly looking round*) I think this is not so bad a place after all when you come to look at it ! A little high up, I grant you, but so quiet and free from intrusion. (*faint knock L. 1 E. D.*) Eh ? (*turns slightly*) Ah ! smoke is the best friend ! Do you know I rally wish you could take a pipe with me, Lucy ! You'll find it such a comfort !

LUCY (*smiling sadly*). Oh, Uncle, the idea of my smoking !

GARNER (*shaking his head*). I don't know about that, my dear ; I hear it's beginning to be the fashion in the tip-toppest society. You see the old women at the apple-stands enjoying their pipe. It's only the extremes meeting, rich and poor—high and low ! (*knock louder, L. 1 E. D.*)

LUCY. I know that knock ! It's Uncle Ben's tap ! (*rises.*)

GARNER. No, my dear, Uncle Ben's tap is a great deal nearer the public-house !

BEN (*puts his head in L. 1 E. D.*) May I come in ?

GARNER. Come in.

Enter BEN, *to* L. C. *slowly.*

On-tray, on-tray ! as the French say !

BEN (*to* LUCY). Come and kiss your poor old nunkey.

LUCY (*going up R. C. to avoid him, taking tea things to cupboard*). I am very busy—very busy—and Uncle is much occupied ! [*Exit, R. 1 E. D. after putting things away.*)

BEN (*whining, looking up R. after* LUCY). She don't want to welcome her old nunkey. Pride, Michael, haughty pride !

GARNER (*smoking pipe*). Yes, we've got so much to be proud of—especially our relations ! (*looks up significantly and then turns his eyes from* BEN *again.*)

BEN. It's all because of your rise in the world.

GARNER. A rise, yes, from the first-floor to the attic—we can't go *much* loftier !

BEN (*maudlin*). Michael, can you forgive me ! (*takes* GARNER'S *hand, and, to mark his speeches, strikes it on table*) Say you will forgive me !

GARNER. If it will be any satisfaction to you, I say I do forgive you !

BEN (*strikes* GARNER'S *hand down on the table as before*). Oh, bless you, Michael ! (*in bringing the hands down a second time,* GARNER *turns his so that* BEN'S *knuckles strike.*) Bless you !

GARNER. This is a pleasant companion for a wet afternoon ! I should say it would be an uncommon *wet* afternoon when you see him !

BEN (*drunkenly*). The Rules and Reggle—reg—gleggle—guggle (*stammering.*)

GARNER. Rules and Regulations—perhaps ?

BEN. The Rules and Reg—(*with an effort*) gle-ations of the social institution in which I am doomed, I repeat, I am doomed, (*trying to seize on the next word, drunkenly*) doomed——

GARNER. Well, keep on saying "I am doomed!" if it's any relief to you. It sounds like swearing, when it ain't!

BEN. The rules and regulations kept me from coming to see you before——

GARNER. Then hooroar for the rules and regulations !

BEN. Say once more, that you forgive me.

GARNER. Twice more, I forgive you.

BEN. Do you forgive me, Mike, for everything I have done ?

GARNER (*in affected horror*). Why, you haven't been and gone and done everything, have you ? Here's a man that has gone and done everything, and an ungrateful country lets him waste his sweetness in the work'us'. "Oh, Albion ! oh, my country, oh ! "

BEN. Michael, I have done you a great injury. I'm an old willain ! (*falls into chair by table.*)

GARNER. Old you are, but villain is not the proper word for my brother.

BEN. Michael, I've lost my peace of mind. It's preying on my conscience, and driving me to an early grave ! I see my crime before me in all its deformity, in the sere and yellow leaf—in all my sereness and yellowness ! I am going—I am going !

GARNER (*offers his hand*). Good-bye !

BEN. You seem very eager to get rid of me, Mike. (*hand in pocket*) I've brought a little present to you—a slight return for my wrong doing. It is not much, (*produces bottle*) but it's the best I can do for you in the miserable state to which I am condemned.

GARNER (*contemptuously*). Drink gin ?

BEN. It is vulgarly so called, but taken in moderation it is known as juniper. I wanted to bring you something as a return, and that's the only thing that I'm a judge of. (*rises*) Good-bye !

GARNER. Don't hurry yourself.

BEN. Bless you, bless you ! (*goes to* L. 1 E., *slowly.*)

GARNER. (*follows him with candle*). Good-bye.

BEN (*at* L. 1 E. D.) Give my love to Sal ! As for Lucy, she is a little spit-fire ! (*half crying*) Good-bye ! Bless you, bless you ! Oh !

[*Exit* L. 1 E. D.

GARNER (*blows the candle out as if the opening of the door did it*). There's the light out now ! (*calls off* L. 1 E.) Mind the loose stairs at the bottom ! (*closes door and goes up* C. *to put candle on table there*) Ah, Michael Garner ! you've sunk low enough in the world, but you've not sunk so low as drink yet ; (*at table* R. C. *front*) after all, though, it was kindly meant of the old chap.

Moonlight in at window in F., GARNER *seated by fire.*

I wonder what he meant by his maunderings on crime and forgiveness ? It must be a touch of the *trimmings*. There's nothing like the trimmings to turn a man's head. I once had an uncle who had the trimmings ; he used to fancy himself the front door, and wanted his chain on, and to be locked up every night. When latch-keys come into fashion, it regularly broke his heart. (*takes up bottle*) It don't smell bad. (*tastes from bottle*) I don't wonder at Uncle Ben taking a drop, now and then. It's a comfort. and he needs a comfort. (*drinks*) Ah ! brave old Tom ! you warm me like a regular furnace. There's nothing to interfere with you.

where you are going, old Tom! I'm empty! You are like Mr. Alexander Selkirk, on the desert Island, you're "Monarch of all you survey!" (*gets drunk*) "May we never want a friend." (*drinks*) "May the evening's amusement bear the"—"a bottle to give him!" (*about to take up bottle, but draws back his hand*) No! I must have my pipe. (*rises, unsteady of foot to get pipe on mantel, drunken business of taking it by the bowl, and finally breaking it*) Oh, my head is splitting! (*stands reeling*) The room seems waving—waving—waving, like the sea. It's the drink that's done it—it's the drink. And I have had no food—no food for days. I am starving! Michael Garner is starving! (*catches at table not to fall.*) and my wife is there (*waves his hand towards* R. U. E.) dying—the food that might have kept her alive, denied her. It's a bad world, they're all rogues or fools in it. The fools are fools for not being rogues! All is going round again! (*to* C.) I feel as if I was walking on air! (*returns to chair* L. *side of table, and falls into it, head on his breast, with agitated hands. etc.*)

Enter, R. U. E. D., LUCY.

LUCY (*gayly*). Oh, I am so glad that Uncle Ben has gone! (*up* L. C.)

GARNER (*fiercely*). What are you glad that Uncle Ben's gone for! Uncle Ben never did any harm to you, did he? (LUCY *recedes to* L. C. *in surprise*) Because Uncle Ben's in the poor-house is he any the worse for that?

LUCY (*aside*). Oh, this is the final blow! (*clasps her hands*) Why are you not here, Charley?

GARNER. Charley? What are you muttering about Charley?

MRS. GARNER *enters* R. U. E. D. *during the ensuing and stands up* C., *in moonlight, listening.**

Hain't there been enough sacrificed to him?

LUCY (*bewildered*). Uncle, dear Uncle, what does this mean?

GARNER (*furiously*). Do you think I committed that robbery. It's time all this nonsense was put a stop to! It's time this model son, this favorite of the family was shown up in his true colors! (*about to take up bottle.*)

LUCY. Don't take any more of that dreadful stuff, Uncle! It will do you ill! (*plaintively*) You used to do everything I asked of you, Uncle, once! (*kneels to* GARNER *and puts arms about his neck*) Do so now! do so now! (GARNER *pushes the bottle from him*) Dear Uncle. (*embraces* GARNER *and rises.*)

GARNER. I'll not be cajoled by your persuading ways! Do you set yourself up to defend the scapegrace? Know him first, the scamp!

LUCY. Don't!

GARNER. A mean-spirited scoundrel who has brought us all to this, drowned my good name in shame, driven me to drink, broken my heart! He stole from his own mother! He plundered his masters. *My* hands are unstained by guilt! He, Charley, Charley, was the real criminal—my son was the forger and the thief!

MRS. GARNER. Ah! (*prolonged scream ; falls full length.*) LUCY (*turns.*)

GARNER (*not looking round*). Who's that? (*rises*).

LUCY (*lifts up* MRS. GARNER) Aunty, Aunty! dear Aunty!

GARNER. She here! Then all is out at last.

MRS. GARNER. Lucy, don't leave me, don't leave me! What's that I heard? I shall go mad!

	MRS. GARNER.	
GARNER *seated.*		LUCY.
R. C.	C.	L. C.

LUCY. Don't mind Uncle. He is in drink; he don't know what he is saying!

GARNER (*putting on drunkenness*). I'm drunk—I don't know what I am saying. (*goes to R. around table; aside*) All is over! (LUCY *places* MRS. GARNER *in chair vacated by* GARNER) The secret I have kept from her all these many years known to her at last!

MRS. GARNER. Michael, Michael! you didn't mean what you were saying? Tell me you did not!

GARNER. No, no!

LUCY. Uncle did not mean anything by it.

MRS. GARNER. My dear boy was always good, and kind, and honest as the day! (*rises*.)

GARNER (*tremulously*). Yes, he was good, and kind and (*with an effort after pause*) honest. (*he lights candle during following*.)

MRS. GARNER. I thought I heard you say dreadful things of Charley. I thought I heard his name coupled with crime. You didn't mean it, Michael? Sleeping in that lonely room, I thought I saw the face of my dear boy, sadder than ever. He sighed to come back. (*clings to* GARNER c.) Oh, why did you let him go away?

Enter L. 1 E. D., MRS. PELLET.

MRS. PELLET. May I come in?

GARNER. Well, what do you want?

MRS. PELLET. My rent, or my apartments.

LUCY. Mrs. Pellet! Oh, your money will be ready for you—soon. I'll speak to you presently.

MRS. PELLET. Oh, I have had enough of your persuasive ways, miss. Ain't I to speak—me that pays my way?

LUCY (*pushes* MRS. PELLET *to* R. 1 E). Another time, another time.

MRS. PELLET. Another time won't do for me with lodgers that haven't got a penny to bless themselves with. I want's my money or my rooms, my money or my rooms! (*the row continued, while* LUCY *pushes her out and follows her off* L. 1 E. D.)

MRS. G. If I could only see the face of my dear boy, really again, I would die in peace—I would die.

GARNER (*on her* L. *side, cheerfully*). How you talk, Sally. You're not one of the dying sort, you want a mouthful of fresh air—it would regularly make you young again. You shall have it, too, when Bolter comes back.

MRS. G. I fear I have been very selfish, in letting the hours slip by without my sharing in the daily work. Do you know, my dear Michael, that it seems to me, in the midst of our privations, that I never loved you so well before, when we were well off?

GARNER. Not a doubt of it, my love. Young, first love is all very well in its way, but it's like a fire fresh lighted—it sputters, and fizzes, and throws out a lot of sparks and smoke—a deal of smoke. But when in time it settles down to a steady flame, it burns clearer, and gives out a brighter light, and, depend upon it, it is warmer.

MRS. G. Michael!

GARNER. My dear wife! (*they embrace*.)

Enter LUCY, L. 1 E. D., *laughing; gas up gradually to full turn on.*

LUCY. Ha, ha, ha! (*immoderately joyful*.)

GARNER. Hullo! what's the matter? Have you been coming to

blows? Lucy, my girl, it was very wrong of you to pitch into Mother Pellet, for weight was agin you!

LUCY. Ha, ha! I'll have it out directly!

GARNER. I should think you had been having it out!

LUCY. Oh, Aunty——(checks herself) A—a gentleman is come to have a look at the rooms. But you needn't go away.

LUCY lets in CHARLEY, who keeps his face averted L. 1 E. D. and then goes up C. with MRS. GARNER.

This is the gentleman, Uncle! (aside) Can this be true?

GARNER* (to CHARLEY, who has taken chair L. C., front). Sir, you really would oblige us if you could wait a day or two. The truth is, we're very hard up just now——

CHARLEY (gruff voice). That's very awkward!

GARNER. It's very awk'ard on us, sir. We are at starvation point, and it would be very hard to turn us out.

CHARLEY. Starvation?

GARNER. A very good imitation of it then.

CHARLEY. I can stand this no longer! (rises, hat off) Don't you know me?

MRS. GARNER. My boy! (embraces CHARLEY. LUCY puts chair up L. out of the way.)

GARNER. Charley, what does this mean? (R. by head of table.)

CHARLEY. Mean? It means that I have come back to pay all your debts and set you up again in the old shop and home, and to make Lucy my darling wife! (takes LUCY's hand.)

GARNER. Eh? Marry Lucy. Why, your talking of committing bigamy! Ain't you married already?

CHARLEY. Me married? No! Could you think me such a scamp?

GARNER. Oh, I don't know about that! Well, now, I begin to see into this!

(Voice of GASSITT heard off L.) But I tell you I will go in!

CHARLEY. His voice! I have been betrayed by him!

GARNER (aside). I'm getting in the clouds! Charley here, a-standing up so proud and a-looking me in the eye honest-like! I begin to believe he'll turn out all right after all!

Enter, L. 1 E. D., GASSITT, surprised at seeing so many in the room, but not recognizing CHARLEY.

GASSITT. Hullo!

GARNER. Hullo yourself, and ever so many more hullos on top of them, and one more little hullo to finish off with! (hands on his hips, arms akimbo, confronts GASSITT) Well, what do you want?

GASSITT. Your—your landlady tells me——

GARNER. My landlady! You let my landlady alone! Mother Pellet is old enough and ugly enough to look after herself, and has no need of an honorary secretary!

GASSITT. Very well, then, I——

GARNER. Go and interfere with your own landlady! Or is it part of your profession as the Honorary Secretary of the Associated Landlady's Antedeluvian Benevolent Society?

---

* MRS. GARNER. LUCY.	
GARNER.	CHARLEY (seated L. C., front.
R. C. C.	L. C.

GASSITT. I want to speak to you, Lucy.

GARNER (*getting before* GASSITT). Who are you calling "Lucy?" I'd like you to know that that young lady's name is Miss Garner, which it will continue to be so when she changes it, and the reason she won't change it when she does change it, is because she's going to marry my son and be more than ever in the family.

GASSITT. Is she? He's already married!

CHARLEY (*advances*). That is false!

GARNER. What do you say to that, Mr. Honorary Secretary?

GASSITT (*recovers himself*). Charley, you have come back! (*sneers*) Ain't you afraid?

CHARLEY. Of what?

GASSITT. Of what generally alarms the thief and the forger—arrest!

CHARLEY. That is all over. But you! how is it I find my family in poverty? where's the money I sent you for them?

GASSITT. I never had it!

CHARLEY. Why did you send me receipts then?

GARNER. Hullo! money sent home to us by Charley! (*arms akimbo again*) Mr. Honorary Secretary, things look fishy! We never had the money!

GASSITT. I couldn't find them before. (*sullenly.*)

GARNER. And you was always a-coming to see us? Oh, no ' I begin to think you are not coming out of this with hands as clean as an honorary secretary should!

GASSITT. Another insult! and I'll let your mother know——

CHARLEY. She does know all about it.

Enter, L. 1 E. D., BEN.

GASSITT. What! that you, not content with forging and bleeding your father, broke open the strong box and stole the savings of your mother like the meanest, vilest, paltriest thief——

CHARLEY. Scoundrel! you lie! (*restrained by* LUCY.)

GARNER. No fighting, Charley! (*to* GASSITT) He says you lie!

GASSITT. You ought to know.

GARNER. Then I should say you do!

BEN (*comes to* L. C.).* He does.

ALL (*except* GASSITT). Uncle Ben!

GARNER. How do you come, I thought the Rules and Regulations——

BEN (*snaps fingers*). That for the Rules and Reggleations! What are Rules and Reggleations to a guilty mind! I took the money! I knew Sally was saving up a trifle for her poor brother-in-law! So, one day when the temptation was too much for my grey hairs, I broke open the box and took the money.

ALL. Ah!

BEN. I am not long for this world—do forgive me.

GARNER. Why you lucky, old, harmless, disgraceful man! I have a mind to knock your venerable old head against that venerable old wall! Get out of the way—I'll speak to you bye-and-bye. (BEN *goes up* L. *To* GASSITT) Now, then, where's the money you had for us?

GASSITT. Spent! The last remittance went to pay my passage out to Bungaroo.

GARNER. What's Bungaroo?

*MRS. G.	CHARLEY.	LUCY.	
	GARNER.	BEN.	GASSITT.
R. C.	C.	L. C.	L.

GASSITT. On the West Coast of Africa.

GARNER. Mr. Gassitt, you have done us all the injury that was in your power. You can do us a great favor—will you ?

GASSITT. What is it ?

GARNER. Take Uncle Ben out to Bungaroo with you! You won't? Then don't let's see your physimahogny any more. (*forces* GASSITT *to* L. 1 R.) Don't you stop to make any long speeches. The stairs are steep and Charley's boot-toes are sharp ?

GASSITT (*at* L. 1 R.) Any commissions for Bungaroo ?

GARNER. No; my compliments to Mr. Bungaroo ! (*turns from door, after* GASSITT *goes out, and then calls off*) And my compliments to Mother Pellet, and she can put the card up in the window—we shan't want her rooms in a hurry again.

MRS. GARNER. My good husband !

GARNER. My dear wife ! (*embraces* MRS. GARNER) The clouds were thick for a while, but the storm has blown over at last, after teaching us the lesson that we should have a kindly word for our friends, who can help us so much in this world by their smiles and their cheerful looks, which are to us DEARER THAN LIFE.

GARNER *and* MRS. GARNER *hand in hand,* L. *of* C., LUCY *and* CHARLEY,
hand in hand, R. *of* C.

CURTAIN.

EXPLANATION OF THE STAGE DIRECTIONS.

The Actor is supposed to face the Audience.

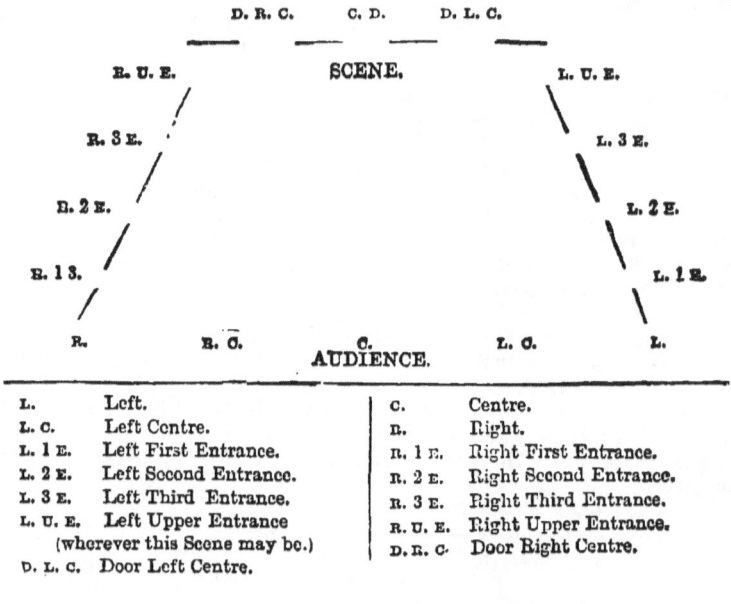

L.	Left.	C.	Centre.
L. C.	Left Centre.	R.	Right.
L. 1 E.	Left First Entrance.	R. 1 R.	Right First Entrance.
L. 2 E.	Left Second Entrance.	R. 2 E.	Right Second Entrance.
L. 3 E.	Left Third Entrance.	R. 3 E.	Right Third Entrance.
L. U. E.	Left Upper Entrance	R. U. E.	Right Upper Entrance.
	(wherever this Scene may be.)	D. R. C.	Door Right Centre.
D. L. C.	Door Left Centre.		

—"Sweetest Shakespeare, Nature's child,
Warbles his native wood-notes wild."—MILTON.

☞ *Please notice that nearly all the Comedies, Farces and Comediettas in the following List of "De Witt's Acting Plays" are very suitable for representation in small Amateur Theatres and on Parlor Stages, as they need but little extrinsic aid from complicated scenery or expensive costumes. They have attained their deserved popularity by their droll situations, excellent plots, great humor and brilliant dialogues, no less than by the fact that they are the most perfect in every respect of any edition of Plays ever published either in the United States or Europe, whether as regards purity of the text, accuracy and fulness of stage directions and scenery, or elegance of typography and clearness of printing.*

*** In ordering, please copy the figures at the commencement of each piece, which indicate the number of the piece in "DE WITT'S LIST OF ACTING PLAYS."

☞ Any of the following Plays sent, postage free, on receipt of price—fifteen cents.

Address, 'ROBERT M. DE WITT,
No. 33 Rose Street, New York.

DE WITT'S ACTING PLAYS.

No.

1 CASTE. An original Comedy in three acts, by T. W.
Robertson. A lively and effective satire upon the times, played successfully in America, at Wallack's. Five male and three female characters. Costumes, modern. Scenery, the first and third acts, interior of a neat room; the second a fashionable room. Time in representation, two hours and forty minutes.

2 NOBODY'S CHILD. A romantic Drama in three acts, by
Watts Phillips. Eighteen male and three female characters. A domestic drama, wonderfully successful in London, as it abounds in stirring scenes and capital situations. Costumes modern, suited to rural life in Wales. Scenery is wild and picturesque. Time in representation, two hours and a quarter.

3 £100,000. An original Comedy in three acts, by Henry J.
Byron. Eight male and four female characters. A most effective piece, played with applause at Wallack's. Costumes of the day. Two scenes are required—a comfortably furnished parlor and an elegant apartment. Time in representation, one hour and three quarters.

No.

4 DANDELION'S DODGES. A Farce in one act, by Thomas J. Williams. Four male and two female characters. A rattling piece. The part of Dandelion excellent for a low comedian. Costumes of the day. Scenery, a picturesque landscape. Time in representation, fifty minutes.

5 WILLIAM TELL WITH A VENGEANCE; or, the Pet, the Patriot and the Pippin. A grand new Burlesque by Henry J. Byron. Eight male and two female characters. Replete with telling allusions. Costumes of the period of the middle ages, grotesquely exaggerated. Five scenes in Switzerland. Time in representation, one hour.

6 SIX MONTHS AGO. A Comedietta in one act, by Felix Dale. Two male and one female characters. A really effective little piece, suited to amateurs. Costumes of the day. Scene, morning room in a country house. Easily produced. Time in representation, forty minutes.

7 MAUD'S PERIL. A Drama in four acts, by Watts Phillips. Five male and three female characters. Strong and sensational. Costume of English country life of the period. Scenery not elaborate. Time in representation, two hours and a half.

8 HENRY DUNBAR; or, a Daughter's Trials. A Drama in four acts, by Tom Taylor. Ten male and three female characters. One of the best acting plays of the day. Costumes of the period. Scenery modern English. Time in representation, three hours.

9 A FEARFUL TRAGEDY IN THE SEVEN DIALS. A farcical interlude in one act, by Charles Selby. Four male and one female characters. A very laughable piece, easily produced; certain to bring down the house. Costumes of the day. Scene, a genteelly furnished bedroom. Time in representation, forty minutes.

10 THE SNAPPING TURTLES; or, Matrimonial Masque- rading. A duologue in one act, by John B. Buckstone. One male and one female character, who assume a second each. A very ludicrous farce; has been eminently successful. Costumes of the day. Scene, a drawing room. Time in representation, one hour.

11 WOODCOCK'S LITTLE GAME. A Comedy Farce in two acts, by J. Maddison Morton. Four male and four female characters. A sparkling, lively composition, by one of the most humorous dramatic authors. The part of Woodcock has been performed by Charles Mathews and Lester Wallack. Costumes of the period. Scenery, modern apartments, handsomely furnished. Time in representation, one hour.

12 A WIDOW HUNT. An original Comedy in three acts, by J. Sterling Coyne. Four male and four female characters. An ingenious and well known alteration of the same author's "Everybody's Friend," the part of Major Wellington de Boots having been rendered popular by Mr. J. S. Clarke in England and America. Costumes and scenery of the period. Time in representation, two hours and a half.

13 RUY BLAS. A romantic Drama in four acts, from the French of Victor Hugo. Twelve male and four female characters. This piece was eminently successful in London when produced by Mr. Fechter. It contains numerous scenes, capable of being performed unconnected with the drama, by amateurs. Spanish costumes of 1692. Scenery, halls and apartments in the royal palace at Madrid. Time in representation, three hours and a half.

14 NO THOROUGHFARE. A Drama in five acts, with a prologue, by Charles Dickens and Wilkie Collins. Thirteen male and six female characters. Very successful as produced by Fechter in England and by Florence in America. Costumes modern but often changed. Scenery complicated; English exteriors, Swiss interiors and Alpine passes. Time in representation, three hours and forty minutes.

15 MILKY WHITE. A domestic Drama in two acts by H. T. Craven. Four male and two female characters. A good acting, pathetic piece. Costumes English, of the present day. Scenery, an exterior and interior. Time in representation, one hour and a half.

DE WITT'S ACTING PLAYS.

No.

16 DEARER THAN LIFE. A serio-comic Drama in three acts, by Henry J. Byron. Six male and five female characters. An effective piece, which could be readily performed by amateurs with success. Costumes, English of the day. Scenery, two interiors, easily arranged. Time in representation, two hours.

17 KIND TO A FAULT. An original Comedy in two acts, by William Brough. Six male and four female characters. A well written composition with well drawn characters. Costumes of the present day. Scenery, two elegantly furnished interiors. Time in representation, one hour and twenty minutes.

18 IF I HAD A THOUSAND A YEAR. A Farce in one act, by John Maddison Morton. Four male and three female characters. A splendid social sketch—the part of Green being excel ent for a good light comedian. Costumes of the present day ; and scenery, a neatly furnished interior. Time in representation, one hour and fifteen minutes.

19 HE'S A LUNATIC. A Farce in one act, by Felix Dale. Three male and two female characters. A sprightly, laughter-provoking production. Modern dresses ; and scene, a drawing room. T me in representation, forty minutes.

20 DADDY GRAY. A serio-comic Drama in three acts, by Andrew Halliday. Eight male and four female characters. One of the author's most effective and natural compositions. Dresses of the present day. Scenery, interior of a cottage, a lawyer's office, street and archway, and cottage with landscape. Time in representation, two hours.

21 DREAMS ; or, My Lady Clara. A Drama in five acts, by T. W. Robertson. Six male and three female characters. Full of thrilling incidents, with several excellent parts for both male and female. Was successfully brought out at the Boston Museum and New York Fifth Avenue Theatre. Costumes, modern German and English. Scenery, interiors and gardens, rather complicated, but effective.

22 DAVID GARRICK. A Comedy in three acts, by T. W. Robertson. Eight male and three female characters. Most effectively performed by Mr. Sothern in England and in America with decided success. Costumes, court dresses. Scenery, two interiors antiquely furnished. Time in representation, one hour and three quarters.

23 THE PETTICOAT PARLIAMENT. An Extravaganza in one act, by Mark Lemon. Fifteen male and twenty-four female characters. A revision of the "House of Ladies." Performed with great success at Mitchell's Olympic in New York. The costumes are extremely fanciful and exaggerated. Scenery, modern English. Time in representation, one hour and five minutes.

24 CABMAN No. 93; or, Found in a Four Wheeler. A Farce in one act, by Thomas J. Williams. Two male and two female characters. A ludicrous piece, with a cabman for the first low comedian, and a stock broker as eccentric character part. Costumes of present day. Scene, a furnished room. Time in representation, forty minutes.

25 THE BROKEN HEARTED CLUB. A Comedietta, by J. Sterling Coyne. Four male and eight female characters. A laughable satire on the Women's Rights movement. Costumes modern English. Scenery, a drawing room. Time in representation, thirty minutes.

26 SOCIETY. A Comedy in three acts, by T. W. Robert- son. Sixteen male and five female characters. A play exceedingly popular, intended to exhibit the foibles of British Society and to ridicule the election system. Costumes of the present day. Scenery elaborate. Time in representation, two hours and a half.

27 TIME AND TIDE. A Drama in three acts and a pro- logue, by Henry Leslie. Seven male and five female characters. An effective piece, with novel and striking incidents. Costumes English, present day. Scenery, London marine scenery. Time in representation, two hours.

DE WITT'S ACTING PLAYS.

No.

28 A HAPPY PAIR. A Comedietta in one act, by S. Theyre Smith. One male and one female character. A neat dramatic sketch of a conjugal misunderstanding. Modern dresses. Scene, a drawing room. Time in representation, twenty minutes.

29 TURNING THE TABLES. A Farce in one act, by John Poole. Five male and three female characters. One of the happiest efforts of the famous author of "Paul Pry." The part of Jeremiah Bumps is redolent with quaint humor. A standard acting piece. Dresses and scenery of the present day. Time in representation, sixty-five minutes.

30 THE GOOSE WITH THE GOLDEN EGGS. A Farce in one act, by Augustus Mayhew and Sutherland Edwards. Five male and three female characters. Gay, rollicking, full of incessant action, having three of the most comical characters imaginable. Costumes of the present period. Scene, a lawyer's office. Time in representation, forty-five minutes.

31 TAMING A TIGER. A Farce in one act, altered from the French. Three male characters. In this a dashing light comedian and fiery, petulant old man cannot fail to extort applause. Modern dresses; and scene, a modern apartment. Time in representation, twenty five minutes.

32 THE LITTLE REBEL. A Farce in one act, by J. Ster- ling Coyne. Four male and three female characters. An excellent piece for a sprightly young actress. Dresses and scenery of the present day. Easy of production. Time in representation, about forty-five minutes.

33 ONE TOO MANY FOR HIM. A Farce in one act, by Thomas J. Williams. Two male and three female characters. Adapted from a popular French vaudeville. Costume of the time. Scene, parlor in country house. Time of representation, fifty minutes.

34 LARKIN'S LOVE LETTERS. A Farce in one act, by Thomas J. Williams. Three male and two female characters. The piece has excellent parts for first low comedy—first old man and a soubrette. Dresses of the day. Scene, a parlor. Time in representation, forty minutes.

35 A SILENT WOMAN. A Farce in one act, by Thomas Hailes Lacy. Two male and one female characters. One of the prettiest little pieces on the English stage. Dresses of the period. Scene, a drawing room. Time in representation, thirty-five minutes.

36 BLACK SHEEP. a Drama in three acts, from Edmund Yates' novel of the same name, and arranged for the stage by J. Palgrave Simpson and the author. Seven male and five female characters. Costumes of the present time. Scenery, an interior; gardens at Homburg, and a handsome parlor. Time in playing, two and a half hours.

37 A SILENT PROTECTOR. A Farce in one act by Thom- as J. Williams. Three male and two female characters. An active, bustling piece of ingenuity, which affords abundant opportunities for the display of Quickfidget's eccentricities. Costumes of the period. Scene, a drawing room. Time in representation, forty minutes.

38 THE RIGHTFUL HEIR. A Drama in five acts, by Lord Lytton (Sir Edward Lytton Bulwer). Ten male and two female characters. A revision and improvement of the author's play of the "Sea Captain," originally produced under management of Mr. Macready. Costumes of the English Elizabethan period, armor, doublets, tights, &c. Scenery picturesque and elaborate. The play contains numerous scenes and passages, which could be selected for declamation. Time in representation, two hours and forty-five minutes.

39 MASTER JONES' BIRTHDAY. A Farce in one act, by John Maddison Morton. Four male and two female characters. A very amusing and effective composition, particularly suited to amateurs. Dresses of the day; and scene, a plain interior. Time of playing, thirty minutes.

40 ATCHI. A Comedietta in one act, by John Maddison Morton. Three male and two female characters. A gem in pleasantry, whose conclusion is irresistibly comic. Costume of the day. Scene, a tastefully laid out garden. Time in representation, forty minutes.

No.

41 BEAUTIFUL FOREVER. A Farce in one act, by Frederick Hay. Two male and two female characters. A sprightly satirical rebuke to those that patronize advertised nostrums. Costumes of the day. Scene, a handsome interior. Time in representation, forty minutes.

42 TIME AND THE HOUR. A Drama in three acts, by J Palgrave Simpson and Felix Dale. Seven male and three female characters. An excellent acting play, full of life and incident, the parts of Medlicott and Marian Beck being capable of impressive representation—all others good. Costumes of the present period. Scenery, gardens and exterior, cottage and garden, and an old oaken chamber. Time in representation, two hours and a half.

43 SISTERLY SERVICE. An original Comedietta in one act, by J. P. Wooler. Seven male and two female characters. An interesting piece. Costumes, rich dresses of the musketeers of Louis XIII. Scenes, an apartment of that period, and a corridor in the royal palace of France. Time in representation, forty minutes.

44 WAR TO THE KNIFE. a Comedy in three acts, by Henry J. Byron. Five male and four female characters. A pleasing, entertaining and morally instructive lesson as to extravagant living; capitally adapted to the stage. Costumes of the present time. Scenes, three interiors. Time in representation, one hour and three quarters.

45 OUR DOMESTICS. A Comedy Farce in two acts, by Frederick Hay. Six male and six female characters. An irresistibly facetious exposition of high life below stairs, and of the way in which servants treat employers during their absence. Costumes of the day. Scenes, kitchen and dining room. Time in representation, one hour and a half.

46 MIRIAM'S CRIME. A Drama in three acts, by H. T. Craven. Five male and two female characters. One of the best acting plays, and easily put on the stage. Costumes modern. Scenery, modern English interiors, two in number. Time in representation, two hours.

47 EASY SHAVING. A Farce in one act, by F. C. Burnand and Montagu Williams. Five male and two female characters. A neat and effective piece, with excellent parts for low comedian and singing chamber maid. Costumes of the days of Charles II of England. Scene, a barber's shop. Time in representation, twenty-five minutes.

48 LITTLE ANNIE'S BIRTHDAY. An original personation Farce, by W. E. Suter. Two male and four female characters. A good farce, whose effectiveness depends upon a singing young lady, who could make the piece a sure success. Costumes modern. Scene, an apartment in an English country house. Time in representation, twenty-five minutes.

49 THE MIDNIGHT WATCH. A Drama in one act, by J. Maddison Morton. Eight male and two female characters. A successful little play. Costumes of the time of the French Revolution of 1795. Scene, the platform of a fortress. Time in representation, one hour.

50 THE PORTER'S KNOT. A serio-comic Drama in two acts, by John Oxenford. Eight male and two female characters. Interesting and thoroughly dramatic. Costumes of the day. Scenes, an interior of cottage and exterior of seaside hotel. Time in representation, one hour and a quarter.

51 A MODEL OF A WIFE. A Farce in one act, by Alfred Wigan. Three male and two female characters. Most amusing in conception and admirably carried out. Costumes of the day. Scene, a painter's studio. Time in representation, thirty-five minutes.

52 A CUP OF TEA. A Comedietta in one act. Translated from the French of *Une Tasse de Thé*, by Charles Nuttier and J. Derley. Three male and one female characters. An exquisite petty comedy, well adapted for amateur representation. Costumes modern. Scene, handsome drawing room. Time in representation, thirty minutes.

DE WITT'S ACTING PLAYS.

DE WITT'S ACTING PLAYS.

No.

89 AUNT CHARLOTTE'S MAID. A Farce in one act, by J. Maddison Morton. Three male and three female characters. One of the best of this prolific humorist's dramatic pieces. Dresses of the period, and scene an apartment in a dwelling house. Time in representation, forty minutes.

90 ONLY A HALFPENNY. A Farce in one act. by John Oxenford. Two male and two female characters. Dresses of the present day, and scene an elegantly furnished interior. Time in representation, thirty-five minutes.

91 WALPOLE; or, Every Man has his Price. A Comedy in rhyme, by Lord Lytton. Seven male and two female characters. Costumes of the period of George I of England. Scenery illustrative of London localities, and residences of the same era. Time of playing, one hour and ten minutes.

92 MY WIFE'S OUT. A Farce in one act, by G. Herbert Rodwell. Two male and two female characters. This piece had a successful run at the Covent Garden Theatre, London. Costume modern, and scene an artist's studio. Time in representation, forty minutes.

93 THE AREA BELLE. A Farce in one act, by William Brough and Andrew Halliday. Three male and two female characters. Costumes of the present time, and scene a kitchen. Time in performing, thirty minutes.

94 OUR CLERKS; or, No. 3, Fig Tree Court, Temple. An original Farce, in one act. Seven male and five female characters. Costumes modern, and scene a large sitting room solidly furnished. Time in representation, sixty-five minutes.

95 THE PRETTY HORSE BREAKER. A Farce, by Wil- liam Brough and Andrew Halliday. Three male and ten female characters. Costumes modern English, and scene a breakfast room in a fashionble mansion. Time of playing, forty-five minutes.

96 DEAREST MAMMA. A Comedietta in one act, by Wal- ter Gordon. Four male and three female characters. Costume modern English, and scene a drawing room. Time in representation, one hour.

97 ORANGE BLOSSOMS. A Comedietta in one act, by J. P. Wooler. Three male and three female characters. Costume of the present day, and scene, a garden with summer house. Time in playing, fifty minutes.

98 WHO IS WHO? or, All in a Fog. A Farce, adapted from the French, by Thomas J. Williams. Three male and two female characters. Costumes, modern English dresses, as worn by country gentry; and scene, parlor, in an old fashioned country house. Time of playing, thirty minutes.

99 THE FIFTH WHEEL. A Comedy in three acts. Ten male and two female characters. An excellent American production, easily managed. Costumes of the modern day. Scenery not complicated. Time of representation, about one hour and three quarters.

100 JACK LONG. A Drama in two acts, by J. B. John- stone. Nine male and two female characters. Costume of the frontiers. Scenery illustrative of localities on the Texan frontier. Time of performance, one hour and twenty minutes.

101 FERNANDE; or, Forgive and Forget. A Drama in three acts, by Victorien Sardou. Eleven male and ten female characters. This is a correct version of the celebrated play as performed in Paris and adapted to the English stage, by Henry L. Williams. Jr. Costumes, modern French. Scenery, four interiors. Time in representation, three hours.

102 FOILED; or, a Struggle for Life and Liberty. A Drama in four acts, by O. W. Cornish. 9 males, 3 females. Costumes, modern American. Scenery—a variety of scenes required, but none elaborate. Time in representation, three and a half hours.

DE WITT'S ACTING PLAYS.

No.

103 FAUST AND MARGUERITE. A romantic Drama in three acts, translated from the French of Michel Carre, by Thomas William Robertson. Nine male and seven female characters. Costumes German, of the sixteenth century; doublets, trunks, tights. Scenery, a laboratory, tavern, garden, street and tableau. Time in representation, two hours.

104 NO NAME. A Drama in five acts, by Wilkie Collins. Seven male and five female characters. A dramatization of the author's popular novel of the same name. Costumes of the present day. Scenery, four interiors and a sea view. Time in representation, three hours.

105 WHICH OF THE TWO. A Comedietta in one act, by John M. Morton. Two male and ten female characters. A very neat and interesting petty comedy. Costume Russian. Scene, public room of an Inn. Time of playing, fifty minutes.

106 UP FOR THE CATTLE SHOW. A Farce in one act, by Harry Lemon. Six male and two female characters. Costumes English, of the present day. Scene, a parlor. Time in representation, forty minutes.

107 CUPBOARD LOVE. A Farce in one act, by Frederick Hay. Two male and one female characters. A good specimen of broad comedy. Dresses modern, and scene, a neatly furnished apartment. Time in representation, twenty minutes.

108 MR. SCROGGINS; or, Change of Name. A Farce in one act, by William Hancock. Three male and three female characters. A lively piece. Costumes of the present day. Scene, a drawing room. Time in representation, forty minutes.

109 LOCKED IN. A Comedietta in one act, by J. P. Wooler. Two male and two female characters. Costumes of the period. Scene, a drawing room. Time in representation, thirty minutes.

110 POPPLETON'S PREDICAMENTS. A Farce in one act, by Charles M. Rae. Three male and six female characters. Costumes of the day. Scene, a drawing room. Time in representation, forty minutes.

111 THE LIAR. A Comedy in two acts, by Samuel Foote. Seven male and two female characters. One of the best acting plays in any language. Costumes, embroidered court dresses, silk sacques, &c; still the modern dress will suffice. Scenes—one, a park, the other a drawing room. Time in representation, one hour and twenty minutes. This edition, as altered by Charles Mathews, is particularly adapted for amateurs.

112 NOT A BIT JEALOUS. A Farce in one act, by T. W. Robertson. Three male and three female characters. Costumes of the day. Scene, a room. Time of playing, forty minutes.

113 CYRIL'S SUCCESS. A Comedy in five acts, by Henry J. Byron. Ten male and four female characters. Costumes modern. Scenery, four interiors. Time in representation, three hours twenty minutes.

114 ANYTHING FOR A CHANGE. A petite Comedy in one act, by Shirley Brooks. Three male and three female characters. Costumes present day. Scene, an interior. Time in representation, fifty-one minutes.

115 NEW MEN AND OLD ACRES. A Comedy in three acts by Tom Taylor. Eight male and five female characters. Costumes present day. Scenery somewhat complicated. Time in representation, two hours.

116 I'M NOT MESILF AT ALL. An original Irish Stew in one act, by C. A. Maltby. Three male and two female characters. Costume of present day, undress uniform, Irish peasant and Highland dress. Scene, a room. Time in playing twenty-eight minutes.

No.

117 NOT SUCH A FOOL AS HE LOOKS. A farcical Drama in three acts, by Henry J. Byron. Five male and four female characters. Excellent for amateurs. Costumes of the day. Scenery, three interiors. Time in representation, two hours.

118 WANTED, A YOUNG LADY. A Farce in one act, by W. E. Suter. Three male characters. Effective for amateurs. Costumes of the day. Scene, a room. Time in playing, forty minutes.

119 A LIFE CHASE. A Drama in five acts, by Adolph Belot; translated by John Oxenford and Horace Wigan. Fourteen male and five female characters. Costumes modern French. Scenery elaborate. Time in representation. two hours and twenty minutes.

120 A TEMPEST IN A TEAPOT. Petite Comedy in one act. Two male and one female characters. Admirably adapted for private performance. Costumes of the day. Scene, an interior. Time of representation, thirty-five minutes.

121 A COMICAL COUNTESS. A Farce in one act, by William Brough. Three male and one female characters. Costumes French, of last century. Scene, a drawing room. Time in representation, forty minutes.

122 ISABELLA ORSINI. A romantic Drama in four acts, by S. H. Mosenthal. Eleven male and four female characters. Costumes Italian, three hundred years ago. Scenery complicated. Time in representation, three and a half hours.

123 THE TWO POLTS. A Farce in one act, by John Courtney. Four male and four female characters. Costumes modern. Scenery, a street and two interiors. Time in representation, forty-five minutes.

124 THE VOLUNTEER REVIEW; or, The Little Man in Green. A Farce in one act, by Thomas J. Williams. Six male and six female characters. Easily localized, as the "Home Guard," or "Militia Muster." Costumes of the day; and scene, a room. Time in representation, forty-five minutes.

125 DEERFOOT. A Farce in one act, by T. C. Burnand. Five male and one female characters. Costumes of the day; and scene, a public house. Time in playing, thirty-five minutes.

126 TWICE KILLED. A Farce in one act, by John Ox- enford. Six male and three female characters. Costumes modern; scene, landscape and a drawing room. Time in playing, forty-five minutes.

127 PEGGY GREEN. A Farce in one act, by Charles Selby. Three male and ten female characters. Costumes of the present day. Scene, a country road. Time in representation, forty-five minutes.

128 THE FEMALE DETECTIVE; or, The Mother's Dying Child. A Drama in three acts, by C. H. Hazlewood. Eleven male and four female characters. Costumes of fifty years since. Scenery very elaborate. Time of playing two hours.

129 IN FOR A HOLIDAY. A Farce in one act, by F. C. Burnand. Two male and three female characters. Costumes of the period, and scene an interior. Time in performance, thirty-five minutes.

130 MY WIFE'S DIARY. A Farce in one act. From the French of MM. Dennery and Clairville, by T. W. Robertson. Three male and one female characters. Costumes modern French, and scene a drawing room. Time in representation, fifty minutes.

131 GO TO PUTNEY. A Farce in one act, by Harry Lemon. Four male and three female characters. Excellent for amateurs. Costumes of the day; scene, a drawing room. Time in representation, forty-five minutes.

DE WITT'S ACTING-PLAYS.

DE WITT'S ACTING PLAYS.

No.

158 SCHOOL. A Comedy in four acts, by T. W. Robertson. Six male and six female characters. Is a very superior piece, and has three characters unusually good for either sex. Could be played with fine effect at a girls' seminary. Costumes modern. Scenery, English landscape and genteel interiors. Time in representation, two hours and forty minutes.

159 IN THE WRONG HOUSE. A Farce in one act, by Martin Becher. Four male and two female characters. A very justly popular piece. Two of the male characters are excellent for light and low comedian. Good parts, too, for a young and old lady. Costumes modern. Scenery, an ordinary room. Time in representation, twenty-five minutes.

160 BLOW FOR BLOW. A Drama in a Prologue and three acts, by Henry J. Byron. Eleven male and six female characters. Full of homely pathos as well as rich humor. Has several excellent parts. Costumes modern. Scenery, interiors of offices and dwellings. Time in representation, three hours.

161 WOMAN'S VOWS AND MASONS' OATHS. In four acts, by A. J. H. Duganne. Ten male and four female characters. Has effective situations, fine characters and beautiful dialogues. Costumes modern, with Federal and Confederate uniforms. Scenery, interiors in country houses, and warlike encampments. Time in performance, two hours and thirty minutes.

162 UNCLE'S WILL. A Comedietta in one act, by S. Theyre Smith. Two male and one female characters. A brilliant piece; can be easily played in a parlor. Costumes modern, and naval uniform for Charles. Scenery, set interior drawing room. Time in representation, thirty minutes.

163 MARCORETTI. A romantic Drama in three acts, by John M. Kingdom. Ten male and three female characters. A thrillingly effective piece, full of strong scenes. Costumes, brigands and rich Italian's dress. Scenery, interior of castle, mountain passes, and princely ball room. Time in representation, two hours.

164 LITTLE RUBY; or, Home Jewels. A domestic Drama in three acts, by J. J. Wallace. Six male and six female characters. This drama is at once affecting and effective. Little Ruby fine personation for young prodigy. Costumes modern. Scenery, interior of dwelling and gardens. Time in representation, two hours.

165 THE LIVING STATUE. A Farce in one act, by Joseph J. Dilley and James Allen. Three male and two female characters. Brimful of fun. Trotter a great character for a droll low comedian. Costumes modern, with one old Roman warrior dress. Scenery, a plain interior.

166 BARDELL vs. PICKWICK. A Farcical sketch in one act, arranged from Charles Dickens. Six male and two female characters. Uncommonly funny. Affords good chance to 'take off" local legal celebrities. Costumes modern. Scenery, a court room. Time in performance, thirty minutes.

167 APPLE BLOSSOMS. A Comedy in three acts, by James Albery. Seven male and three female characters. A pleasing piece, with rich part for an eccentric comedian. Costumes modern English. Scenery, exterior and interior of inn. Time in representation, two hours and twenty minutes.

168 TWEEDIE'S RIGHTS. A Comedy in two acts, by James Albery. Four male and two female characters. Has several excellent characters. John Tweedie, powerful personation; Tim Whiffler very funny. Costumes modern. Scenery, a stone mason's yard and modest interior. Time in representation, one hour and twenty-five minutes.

DE WITT'S ACTING PLAYS.

DE WITT'S ETHIOPIAN AND COMIC DRAMA

"Let those laugh now who never laughed before;
And those who always laughed now laugh the more."

Nothing so thorough and complete in the way of Ethiopian and Comic Dramas has ever been printed as those that appear in the following list. Not only are the plots excellent, the characters droll, the incidents' funny, the language humorous, but all the situations, by-play, positions, pantomimic business, scenery and tricks are so plainly set down and clearly explained, that the merest novice could put any of them on the Stage. Included in this Catalogue are all the most laughable and effective pieces of their class ever produced.

⁎⁎⁎ In ordering, please copy the figures at the commencement of each Play, which indicate the number of the piece in "DE WITT'S ETHIOPIAN AND COMIC DRAMA."

☞ Any of the following Plays sent, postage free, on receipt of price—fifteen cents.

Address as on first page of this Catalogue.

DE WITT'S ETHIOPIAN AND COMIC DRAMA.

No.

1 THE LAST OF THE MOHICANS. An Ethiopian Sketch, by J. C. Stewart. Three male and one female characters. Costumes of the day, except Indian shirts, &c. Two scenes, chamber and wood. Time in representation, eighteen minutes.

2 TRICKS. An Ethiopian Sketch, by J. C. Stewart. Five male and two female characters. Costumes of the period. Two scenes, two interiors. Time in representation, eighteen minutes.

3 HEMMED IN. An Ethiopian Sketch, by J. C. Stewart. Three male and one female characters. Costumes modern, and scene, a studio. Time in representation, twenty minutes.

4 EH? WHAT IS IT? An Ethiopian Sketch, by J. C. Stewart. Four male and one female characters. Costumes of the day, and scene, a chamber. Time in representation, twenty minutes.

5 TWO BLACK ROSES. An Ethiopian Sketch, by J. C. Stewart. Four male and one female characters. Costumes modern, and scene, an apartment. Time in representation, twenty minutes.

No.

6 THE BLACK CHAP FROM WHITECHAPEL. An eccentric Negro Piece, adapted from Burnand and Williams' "B. B" by Henry L. Williams, Jr. Four male characters. Costumes modern. Scene, an interior. Time in representation, thirty minutes.

7 THE STUPID SERVANT. An Ethiopian Sketch in one scene, by Charles White. Two male characters. Characters very droll; fit for star "darky" players. Costumes modern and fantastic dresses. Scenery, an ordinary room. Time in representation, twenty minutes.

8 THE MUTTON TRIAL. An Ethiopian Sketch in two scenes, by James Maffit. Four male characters. Capital burlesque of courts of "justice;" all the parts good. Costumes modern and Quaker. Scenery, a wood view and a court room. Time in representation, twenty minutes.

9 THE POLICY PLAYERS. An Ethiopian Sketch in one scene, by Charles White. Seven male characters. A very clever satire upon a sad vice. Costumes modern, and coarse negro ragged clothes. Scenery, an ordinary kitchen. Time in representation, twenty minutes.

10 THE BLACK CHEMIST. An Ethiopian Sketch in one scene, by Charles White. Three male characters. All the characters are A 1, funny in the extreme. Costumes modern or Yankee-extravagant. Scenery, an apothecary's laboratory. Time in representation, seventeen minutes.

11 BLACK-EY'D WILLIAM. An Ethiopian Sketch in two scenes, by Charles White. Four male, one female characters. All the parts remarkably good. Costumes as extravagant as possible. Scenery, a police court room. Time in representation, twenty minutes.

12 DAGUERREOTYPES. An Ethiopian Sketch in one scene, by Charles White. Three male characters. Full of broad humor; all characters excellent. Costumes modern genteel, negro and Yankee garbs. Scenery, ordinary room with camera. Time in representation, fifteen minutes.

13 THE STREETS OF NEW YORK; or, New York by Gaslight. An Ethiopian Sketch in one scene, by Charles White. Six male characters. Three of the parts very droll; others good. Costumes some modern, some Yankee and some loaferish. Scenery, street view. Time in representation, eighteen minutes.

14 THE RECRUITING OFFICE. An Ethiopian Sketch in one act, by Charles White. Five male characters. A piece full of incidents to raise mirth. Three of the parts capital. Costumes extravagant, white and darkey, and a comical uniform. Scenery, plain chamber and a street. Time in representation, fifteen minutes.

15 SAM'S COURTSHIP. An Ethiopian Farce in one act, by Charles White. Two male and one female characters. All the characters particularly jolly. Two of the parts can be played in either white or black, and one in Dutch. Costumes Yankee and modern. Scenery, plain chamber. Time in representation, twenty minutes.

16 STORMING THE FORT. A burlesque Ethiopian Sketch in one scene, by Charles White. Five male characters. Richly ludicrous; all the characters funny. Costumes fantastical, and extravagant military uniforms. Scenery, ludicrous "take off" of fortifications. Time in representation, fifteen minutes.

17 THE GHOST. An Ethiopian Sketch in one act, by Charles White. Two male characters. A right smart piece, full of laugh. Costumes ordinary "darkey" clothes. Scenery common looking kitchen. Time in representation, fifteen minutes.

18 THE LIVE INDIAN; or, Jim Crow. A comical Ethi- opian Sketch in four scenes, by Dan Bryant. Four male, one female characters. As full of fun as a hedgehog is full of bristles. Costumes modern and darkey. Scenery, chamber and street. Time in representation, twenty minutes.

DE WITT'S ETHIOPIAN AND COMIC DRAMA.

No.

19 **MALICIOUS TRESPASS; or, Points of Law. An Ethi-**opian Sketch in one scene, by Charles White. Three male characters. Extravagantly comical ; all the parts very good. Costumes extravagant modern garbs. Scenery, wood or landscape. Time of playing, twenty minutes.

20 **GOING FOR THE CUP ; or, Old Mrs. Williams' Dance.** An Ethiopian Interlude, by Charles White. Four male characters. One capital part for a bright juvenile ; the others very droll. Costumes modern and darkey. Scenery, a landscape or wood. Time in representation, twenty minutes.

21 **SCAMPINI. An anti-tragical, comical, magical and** laughable Pantomime, full of tricks and transformations, in two scenes, by Edward Warden. Six male, three female characters. Costumes extravagantly eccentric. Scenery, plain rustic chamber. Time in representation, thirty minutes.

22 **OBEYING ORDERS. An Ethiopian Military Sketch in** one scene, by John Arnold. Two male, one female characters. Mary Jane, a capital wench part. The piece very jocose. Costumes ludicrous military and old style dresses. Scenery either plain or fancy chamber. Time of playing, fifteen minutes.

23 **HARD TIMES. A Negro Extravaganza in one scene.** by Daniel D. Emmett. Five male, one female characters. Needs several good players—then there is " music in the air." Costumes burlesque, fashionable and low negro dresses. Scenery, a kitchen. Time in representation, twenty minutes.

24 **BRUISED AND CURED. A Negro Burlesque Sketch in** one scene, by A. J. Leavitt. Two male characters. A rich satire upon the muscular furore of the day. Costumes tights and guernsey shirts and negro dress. Scenery, plain chamber. Time in representation, twenty minutes.

25 **THE FELLOW THAT LOOKS LIKE ME. A laughable** Interlude in one scene, by Oliver Durivarge. Two male characters—one female. Boiling over with fun, especially if one can make up like Lester Wallack. Costumes genteel modern. Scenery, handsome chamber. Time in representation, twenty-five minutes.

26 **RIVAL TENANTS. A Negro Sketch, by George L. Stout.** Four male characters. Humorously satirical ; the parts all very funny. Costumes negro and modern. Scenery, an old kitchen. Time of playing, twenty minutes.

27 **ONE HUNDREDTH NIGHT OF HAMLET. A Negro** Sketch, by Charles White. Seven male, one female characters. Affords excellent chance for imitations of popular "stars." Costumes modern, some very shabby. Scenery, plain chamber. Time in representation, twenty minutes.

28 **UNCLE EPH'S DREAM. An Original Negro Sketch in** two scenes and two tableaux, arranged by Charles White. Three male, one female characters. A very pathetic little piece, with a sprinkling of humor. Costumes, a modern southern dress and negro toggery. Scenery, wood, mansion and negro hut. Time in representation, twenty minutes.

29 **WHO DIED FIRST? A Negro Sketch in one Scene, by** A. J. Leavitt. Three male, one female characters. Jasper and Hannah are both very comical personages. Costumes, ordinary street dress and common darkey clothes. Scenery, a kitchen. Time in representation, twenty minutes.

30 **ONE NIGHT IN A BAR ROOM. A Burlesque Sketch,** arranged by Charles White. Seven male characters. Has a funny Dutchman and two good darkey characters. Costume, one Dutch and several modern. Scenery, an ordinary interior. Time in representation, twenty minutes.

No.

31 GLYCERINE OIL. An Ethiopian Sketch, by John Ar- nold. Three male characters, all good. Costumes, Quaker and eccentric modern. Scenery, a street and a kitchen. Time in representation, fifteen minutes.

32 WAKE UP, WILLIAM HENRY. A Negro Sketch, ar- ranged by Charles White. Three male characters, which have been favor- ites of our best performers. Costumes modern—some eccentric. Scenery plain chamber. Time in representation, ten minutes.

33 JEALOUS HUSBAND. A Negro Sketch, arranged by Charles White. Two male, one female characters. Full of farcical dia- logue. Costumes, ordinary modern dress. Scenery, a fancy rustic cham- ber. Time in representation, twenty minutes.

34 THREE STRINGS TO ONE BOW. An Ethiopian Sketch in one scene, arranged by Charles White. Four male, one female charac- ters. Full of rough, practical jokes. Costumes, modern. Scenery, a land- scape. Time in representation, fifteen minutes.

35 COAL HEAVERS' REVENGE. A Negro Sketch in one scene, by George L. Stout. Six male characters. The two coal heavers have "roaring" parts. Costumes, modern, Irish and negro comic make up. Scenery, landscape. Time in representation, twenty minutes.

36 LAUGHING GAS. A Negro Burlesque Sketch in one scene, arranged by Charles White. Six male, one female characters. Is a favorite with our best companies. Costumes, one modern genteel, the rest ordinary negro. Scenery, plain chamber. Time of playing, fifteen min- utes.

37 A LUCKY JOB. A Negro Farce in two scenes, arranged by Charles White. Three male, two female characters. A rattling, lively piece. Costumes, modern and eccentric. Scenery, street and fancy cham- ber. Time in representation, thirty minutes.

38 SIAMESE TWINS. A Negro Burlesque Sketch, in two scenes, arranged by Charles White. Five male characters. One of the richest in fun of any going. Costumes, Irish, darkey and one wizard's dress. Scenery, a street and a chamber. Time in representation, twenty- five minutes.

39 WANTED A NURSE. A laughable Sketch in one scene, arranged by Charles White. Four male characters. All the charac- ters first rate. Costume, modern, extravagant, one Dutch dress. Scenery, a plain kitchen. Time in representation, twenty minutes.

40 A BIG MISTAKE. A Negro Sketch in one scene, by A. J. Leavitt. Four male characters. Full of most absurdly funny inci- dents. Costumes, modern ; one policeman's uniform. Scenery, a plain chamber. Time in representation, eighteen minutes.

41. CREMATION. An Ethiopian Sketch in two scenes, by A. J. Leavitt. Eight male, one female characters. Full of broad, palpable hits at the last sensation. Costumes modern, some eccentric. Scenery, a street and a plain chamber. Time in representation, twenty-five minutes.

42. BAD WHISKEY. A comic Irish Sketch in one scene, by Sam Rickey and Master Barney. Two male, one female characters. One of the very best of its class. Extravagant low Irish dress and a police- man's uniform.

43 BABY ELEPHANT. A Negro Sketch in two scenes. By J. C. Stewart. Seven male, one female characters. Uproariously comic in idea and execution. Costumes, modern. Scenery, one street, one chamber. Time in representation, twenty-five minutes.

44 THE MUSICAL SERVANT. An Ethiopian Sketch in one scene, by Phil. H. Mowrey. Three male characters. Very original and very droll. Costumes, modern and low darkey. Scenery, a plain chamber. Time in representation, fifteen minutes

No.

45 REMITTANCE FROM HOME. An Ethiopian Sketch in one scene, by A. J. Leavitt. Six male characters. A very lively piece, full of bustle, and giving half a dozen people a good chance. Time in representation, twenty minutes.

46 A SLIPPERY DAY. An Ethiopian Sketch in one scene, by Robert Hart. Six male, one female characters. By a very simple mechanical contrivance, plainly planned and described in this book, a few persons can keep an audience roaring. Time in representation, sixteen minutes.

47 TAKE IT, DON'T TAKE IT. A Negro Sketch in one scene, by John Wild. Two male characters. Affords a capital chance for two good persons to "do" the heaviest kind of deep, deep tragedy. Time of representation, twenty-three minutes.

48 HIGH JACK, THE HEELER. An Ethiopian Sketch in one scene, by A. J. Leavitt. Six male characters. Happily hits off the short-haired bragging "fighters" that can't lick a piece of big taffy. Time of playing, twenty minutes.

49 A NIGHT IN A STRANGE HOTEL. A laughable Negro Sketch in one scene, arranged by Charles White. Two male characters. Although this piece has only two personators, it is full of fun. Time in representation, eighteen minutes.

50 THE DRAFT. A Negro Sketch in one act and two scenes, by Charles White. Six male characters. A good deal of humor of the Mulligan Guard and Awkward Squad style, dramatized. Time in representation, eighteen minutes.

51 FISHERMAN'S LUCK. An Ethiopian Sketch in one scene, by Charles White. Two male characters. Decidedly the best "fish story" ever told. It needs two "star" darkeys to do it. Time in representation, fifteen minutes.

52 EXCISE TRIALS. A Burlesque Negro Sketch in one scene, arranged by Charles White. Ten male, one female characters. Full of strong local satire; can be easily adapted to any locality. Time of representation, twenty minutes.

53 DAMON AND PYTHIAS. A Negro Burlesque, by Chas. White. Five male, one female characters, in two scenes. A stunning burlesque of the highfalutin melodrama; capital for one or two good imitators. Time of representation, fifteen minutes.

54 THEM PAPERS. An Ethiopian Sketch in one scene, by A. J. Leavitt. Three male characters. Full of comical mystifications and absurdly funny situations. Time of representation, fifteen minutes.

55 RIGGING A PURCHASE. A Negro Sketch in one scene, by A. J. Leavitt. Three male characters. Full of broad comical effects. Time in representation, fifteen minutes.

56 THE STAGE STRUCK COUPLE. A laughable Inter- lude in one scene, by Charles White. Two male, one female characters. Gives the comical phase of juvenile dramatic furor; very droll, contrasted with the matter-of-fact darkey. Time in representation, fifteen minutes.

57 POMPEY'S PATIENTS. A laughable Interlude in two scenes, arranged by Charles White. Six male characters. Very funny practical tricks of a fast youth to gain the governor's consent to his wedding his true love. Half a dozen good chances for good actors. Time in representation, twenty minutes.

No.

58 GHOST IN A PAWN SHOP. An Ethiopian Sketch in one scene, by Mr. Mackey. Four male characters. As comical as its title ; running over with practical jokes. Time of representation, twenty minutes.

59 THE SAUSAGE MAKERS. A Negro Burlesque Sketch in two scenes, arranged by Charles White. Five male, one female characters. An old story worked up with a deal of laughable effect. The ponderous sausage machine and other properties need not cost more than a couple of dollars. Time of representation, twenty minutes.

60 THE LOST WILL. A Negro Sketch, by A. J. Leavitt. Four male characters. Very droll from the word "go." Time of representation, eighteen minutes.

61 THE HAPPY COUPLE. A Short Humorous scene, arranged by Charles White. Two male, one female characters. A spirited burlesque of foolish jealousy. Sam is a very frolicsome, and very funny young darkey. Time of playing, seventeen minutes.

62 VINEGAR BITTERS. A Negro Sketch in one scene, arranged by Charles White. Six male, one female characters. A broad burlesque of the popular patent medicine business ; plenty of humorous incidents. Time of representation, fifteen minutes.

63 THE DARKEY'S STRATAGEM. A Negro Sketch in one act, arranged by Charles White. Three male, one female characters. Quaint courtship scenes of a pair of young darkies, ludicrously exaggerated by the tricks of the boy Cupid. Time of representation, twenty minutes.

64 THE DUTCHMAN'S GHOST. In one scene, by Larry Tooley. Four male, one female characters. Jacob Schrochoru, the jolly shoemaker and his frau, are rare ones for raising a hearty laugh. Time of representation, fifteen minutes.

65 PORTER'S TROUBLES. An Amusing Sketch in one scene, by Ed. Harrigan. Six male, one female characters. A laughable exposition of the queer freaks of a couple of eccentric lodgers that pester a poor "porter." Time of representation, eighteen minutes.

66 PORT WINE vs. JEALOUSY. A Highly Amusing Sketch, by William Carter. Two male, one female characters. Twenty minutes jammed full of the funniest kind of fun.

67 EDITOR'S TROUBLES. A Farce in one scene, by Ed- ward Harrigan. Six male characters. A broad farcical description of the running of a country journal "under difficulties." Time of representation, twenty-three minutes.

68 HIPPOTHEATRON OR BURLESQUE CIRCUS. An Extravagant, funny Sketch, by Charles White. Nine male characters. A rich burlesque of sports in the ring and stone smashing prodigies. Time of playing, varies with "acts" introduced.

69 SQUIRE FOR A DAY. A Negro Sketch, by A. J. Leavitt. Five male, one female characters. The "humor of it" is in the mock judicial antics of a darkey judge for a day. Time of representation, twenty minutes.

70 GUIDE TO THE STAGE. An Ethiopian Sketch, by Chas. White. Three male characters. Contains some thumping theatrical hits of the "Lay on Macduff," style. Time of playing, twelve minutes.

MANUSCRIPT PLAYS.

Below will be found a List of nearly all the great Dramatic successes of the present and past seasons. Every one of these Plays, it will be noticed, are the productions of the most eminent Dramatists of the age. Nothing is omitted that can in any manner lighten the duties of the Stage Manager, the Scene Painter or the Property Man.

ON THE JURY. A Drama, in four Acts. By Watts Philips. This piece has seven male and four female characters.

ELFIE; or, THE CHERRY TREE INN. A Romantic Drama, in three Acts. By Dion Boucicault. This piece has six male and four female characters.

THE TWO THORNS. A Comedy, in four Acts. By James Albery. This piece has nine male and three female characters.

A WRONG MAN IN THE RIGHT PLACE. A Farce, in one Act. By John Oxenford. This piece has one male and three female characters.

JEZEBEL; or, THE DEAD RECKONING. By Dion Bou- cicault. This piece has six male and five female characters.

THE RAPAREE; or, THE TREATY OF LIMERICK. A Drama, in three Acts. By Dion Boucicault. This piece has nine male and two female characters.

'TWIXT AXE AND CROWN; or, THE LADY ELIZA- beth. An Historical Play, in five Acts. By Tom Taylor. This piece has twenty-five male and twelve female characters.

THE TWO ROSES. A Comedy, in three Acts. By James Albery. This piece has five male and four female characters.

M. P. (Member of Parliament) A Comedy, in four Acts. By T. W. Robertson. This piece has seven male and five female characters.

MARY WARNER. A Domestic Drama, in four Acts. By Tom Taylor. This piece has eleven male and five female characters.

PHILOMEL. A Romantic Drama, in three Acts. By H. T. Craven. This piece has six male and four female characters.

UNCLE DICK'S DARLING. A Domestic Drama, in three Acts. By Henry J. Byron. This piece has six male and five female characters.

LITTLE EM'LY. (David Copperfield.) A Drama, in four Acts. By Andrew Halliday. "Little Em'ly" has eight male and eight female characters.

DE WITT'S ELOCUTIONARY SERIES.

PRICE 15 CENTS EACH.

Young people who were desirous of acquiring a practical knowledge of the beautiful, as well as highly useful art of Reading and Speaking correctly and elegantly, have found great difficulty in procuring books that would teach them rather in the manner of a ge ial FRIEND *than an imperious* MASTER. *Such books we here present to the public in "De Witt's Elocutionary Series." Not only are the selections made very carefully from the abundant harvest of dramatic literature, but the accompanying* INSTRUCTIONS *are so* PLAIN, DIRECT *and* FORCIBLE, *that the least intelligent can easily understand all the rules and precepts of the glorious art that has immortalized Roscius and Kean, Chatham and Henry.*

No. 1. THE ACADEMIC SPEAKER. Containing an un-usual variety of striking Dramatic Dialogues, and other most effective scenes. Selected with great care and judgment from the noblest and wittiest Dramas, Comedies and Farces most popular upon the best stages. Interspersed with such able, plain and practical criticisms and remarks upon Elocution and stage effects, as to render this work the most valuable hand-book to the young orator that has ever been produced.

CONTENTS.—General Introductory Remarks ; On the quality of Selections ; On True Eloquence ; On Awkward Delivery ; On Necessity of Attentive study ; On Appropriate Gesture ; On the Appearance of Ladies upon the Stage ; The Stage and the Curtain ; Remarks upon the subject of Scenery ; How to easily Construct a Stage ; Stage Arrangements and Properties ; Remarks upon improvising Wardrobes, etc., etc. There are *Twelve* pieces in this book that require *two* Male Characters ; *Six* pieces that require *six* Male Characters ; *Two* pieces that require *four* Male Characters.

No. 2. THE DRAMATIC SPEAKER. Composed of manyvery carefully chosen Monologues, Dialogues and other effective Scenes, from the most famous Tragedies, Comedies and Farces. Interspersed with numerous Directions and Instructions for their proper Delivery and Performance.

CONTENTS.—There are *three* pieces in this book that require *one* Male Character; *One* that requires *three* Male Characters ; *Ten* that require *two* Male Characters , *Nine* that require *one* Male and *one* Female Characters ; *Four* that require *three* Male Characters ; *One* that requires *two* Male and *one* Female Characters ; *One* that requires *two* Female Characters ; *One* that requires *one* Male and *two* Female Characters.

No. 3. THE HISTRIONIC SPEAKER. Being a carefulcompilation of the most amusing Dramatic Scenes, light, gay, pointed, witty and sparkling. Selected from the most elegantly written and most theatrically effective Comedies and Farces upon the English and American Stages. Properly arranged and adapted for Amateur and Parlor Representation.

CONTENTS.—*Three* of the pieces in this book require *two* Female Characters ; *One* piece requires *seven* Female Characters ; *Nineteen* pieces that require *one* Male and *one* Female Characters ; *One* piece that requires *one* Male and *two* Female Characters ; *One* piece that requires *two* Male and *one* Female Characters.

No. 4. THE THESPIAN SPEAKER. Being the best Scenesfrom the best Plays. Every extract is preceded by valuable and very plain observations, teaching the young Forensic Student how to Speak and Act in the most highly approved manner.

CONTENTS.—*Five* of the pieces in this book require *one* Male and *one* Female Characters ; *Three* of the pieces require *three* Male Characters ; *Three* of the pieces require *two* Male and *one* Female Characters ; *Seven* of the pieces require *two* Male Characters ; *One* of the pieces require *one* Male and *one* Female Characters ; *Two* of the pieces require *two* Male and *two* Female Characters ; *One* of the pieces require *four* Male and *four* Female Characters ; *Three* of the pieces require *three* Male and *one* Female Characters.

*** Single copies sent, on receipt of price, postage free.

☞ Address as per first page of this Catalogue.